SIMPLY SMITTEN

BRIDES OF SEATTLE SERIES, BOOK 2

KIMBERLY ROSE JOHNSON

Simply Smitten
Published by Sweet Rose Press
U.S.A.

Edited by Miralee Ferrell
Cover Design Castle Creations
Formatting by Cindy Jackson
Printed in the United States of America

Acknowledgements

I want to take a moment to thank all the people who helped me with this book. You know who you are. I sincerely appreciate your willingness to critique and proofread my work.

1

Hailey O'Brien stared out the window at the forest landscape. The train swayed gently as it chugged along the track toward Seattle—home. It had been four years since she had been there for more than the Christmas holidays, much to her mother's and brother's disappointment. She'd enjoyed attending school in Chicago, but it was time to face her past and move forward into life as an adult.

"Hailey?" A hand waved in front of her face.

She blinked and pulled her thoughts back to the present and the man beside her. "I'm sorry, Michael. What were you saying?" She'd met Michael a week ago at her job interview. When she first saw him she had a moment of panic because he looked like a young version of Josh Duhamel, but she'd quickly recovered thanks to his engaging smile and quick wit that put her at ease. It was because of him she was returning to Seattle gainfully employed—funny that they would meet again on the train. Apparently he avoided flying if at all possible.

"I'm going to buy a snack. Would you like anything?"

"A bag of chocolate-covered almonds would be great." She dug into her oversized purse and pulled out a ten-dollar bill. "Maybe make it two this time."

Michael chuckled. "You have a serious problem."

She nudged his shoulder with hers. "Don't judge me. I'm nervous, and when I'm nervous, I eat chocolate."

"So noted."

"You don't need to be nervous about working for MM Enterprises. It's a great company to work for." He took her money and stood. "I'll be back soon."

"That's not what I'm nervous about," she mumbled to herself. Although now that he mentioned it maybe she should be. How was it at age twenty-four and fresh out of grad school she'd landed her dream job as the economic adviser to the CEO of an up-and-coming software company? She'd be advising them on how to grow their company. According to Michael, with her help, they planned to take the company to the next level. She sure hoped she could live up to their expectations.

She never would have known about the job much less thought to apply, were it not for Ian Parker, her brother's best friend—MM's star software developer. He must have made her sound amazing for them to send Michael to Chicago to interview her. It still boggled her mind that they did that.

She dipped her head back and closed her eyes. But before she started her new job she had to face her family.

It would be so weird living with her brother while apartment hunting. At least Ray and Katie were no longer newlyweds, but they had a full house with three kids, including their eight-year-old niece, so she couldn't overstay her welcome.

Michael strolled down the aisle toward Hailey. Her eyes were closed. He paused and studied her while she was unaware. Her classic beauty reminded him of Anne Hathaway—he'd had a crush on the actress back when she starred in Princess Diaries. His mom used to watch it all the time. He shook away the memory and focused on the present.

Too bad Hailey was his new right hand—they'd be working closely together as his company navigated where and how to expand. He'd have asked her out, but as things were, it would be improper.

Michael cleared his throat as he approached his seat. "Two bags of sugar and protein as requested." He held out the packs as he eased into the seat beside Hailey. He hadn't planned for her to think he was his business partner's assistant, but when she'd made the assumption at her interview, he hadn't corrected her—a decision he regretted. Now they had a rapport going, telling her that he was actually her new boss would ruin that. But it had to be done.

"Thanks. That was fast." She tore open a bag and

poured a few into her hand.

"No line this time. How about you tell me what you're so nervous about? Maybe I can help."

She shook her head, causing her long, dark hair to shift around her shoulders. She met his gaze with her hazel eyes framed by long lashes.

He sucked in a breath. He couldn't be attracted to her, but he could be her friend. Now to get his heart to follow good sense.

"I don't think you can help me with this, but if you really want to listen, I'll tell you."

"I do. Besides, what else is there to do? We have about an hour before we get to Seattle."

"Okay then. But you might regret it. It's a sad story." She shifted to better face him. "I left home a year after my older sister and her husband were killed in a car accident. At the time, I attended the University of Washington, but I had to get out of my mom's house and away from the constant reminder that my sister was gone. My mom's grief as well as my own was too much for me to deal with. So I applied to Northwestern University and moved away that August. Mom was furious that I was leaving her, but it was honestly self-preservation. I had to get out of there." Her gaze dropped to her lap.

The pain in her eyes ripped his gut in two. No one should have to deal with what she had, especially when so young. "I'm sorry about your sister and brother-in-law."

She tilted her head slightly, meeting his gaze.

"Thanks. I'm doing fine now, but I'm nervous about reconnecting with my family. I've only been home for Christmas. My brother and I were closer before I left, but we drifted apart through no fault of his. I shut him out—a choice I now regret. He's the best. He even took in our niece when our sister died and is raising her as his own."

"He sounds like a nice guy who loves his family very much. I don't think you need to worry."

"I'm not too worried about Ray and his family. It's mostly my mom. She's been less than understanding. If it wasn't for my brother I don't think I'd have taken this job, but he supports me one hundred percent."

"I'm glad you have him." Michael thought she would tell him about why she was nervous about the job, not about her personal life. His shoulder muscles tightened to the point if he didn't relax he'd be in desperate need of a massage. Hailey was going to hate him when she learned the truth about him. But for now he'd let her talk since it seemed to be helping her. "Tell me about your brother's family."

"He married his wife shortly after the accident. To be honest, I think he might have rushed the wedding because he was overwhelmed with our niece, who was only four at the time, but whatever the reason he's happy. He and Katie have two other children. A boy and a girl."

"The perfect family." He'd always wanted another brother, but it was only him and his twin brother.

"Yes, they really are. But perfect or not, I want to

find an apartment as fast as possible and get out of their home. I don't want to be the houseguest that never leaves."

He chuckled. "Somehow, I don't think that will be a problem."

"I hope not. The thing I'm most concerned about is it being awkward between us since I took off and left him to deal with our mother."

"Time and distance have a way of changing relationships, but if your brother is the man I suspect he is, I don't think you have anything to worry about." He knew first hand how time and distance affected relationships. It was, after all, the reason he was still single at twenty-nine. He glanced at his watch. It was time to tell her the truth about who he was. If he waited any longer they'd be too close to Seattle, and she wouldn't have time to hear him out.

"I sure hope we can pick up where we left off. I love my niece even from afar. My sister-in-law is a great mom to her too, and my brother really is the best."

"Good." He cleared his throat. "I'm sorry for the abrupt subject change, but we'll be in Seattle soon, and there's something you need to know before we get there."

Wariness filled her hazel eyes, but she masked it with a smile. "You're married, right? I should have known. All the good ones are taken."

He chuckled, but it sounded strangled. "No. I'm single."

Her face lit.

"But...the thing is," he added quickly before this became even more awkward. "I'm the other M in MM Enterprises."

"Are you saying you're my boss?" Her face paled.

He nodded. "And as much as I've enjoyed the time we've had on the ride to Seattle to get acquainted, that's all I can offer on a personal level."

She blinked. "You co-own MM Enterprises?"

"Guilty. Will you forgive me for letting you believe I'm Mason's assistant?"

"Of course, but I wish you would have told me before I bared my soul to you. I've never told anyone all of that."

"I understand, and had I realized you were going to do that, I would have said something sooner. The thing is, when you mistook me for an assistant, it seemed to put you at ease. I didn't have the heart to correct you at the time of your interview."

"Or right after, apparently." Her brow furrowed.

"I hope this won't affect our working relationship."

"Not at all, Mister..." She met his gaze. "I'm sorry, I don't know your last name."

"Pierce. But please keep calling me Michael. We're casual at MM, and we all go by our first names."

She only nodded.

"You're angry."

"I'm not angry, but I feel foolish. I really wish you would've said something sooner." She shifted to look out the window.

"I'm sorry. I realize now I made a poor choice. I'm

an honest person, which I hope you'll discover for yourself. I'd hate for you to quit before you even start."

Her head whipped his direction. "Oh, I'm not quitting. And I could tell you're trustworthy. I suppose we're all entitled to at least one bad decision."

"Thank you. Are we good?"

"We're as good as a new boss and his employee can be. I appreciate you setting the record straight now rather than my first day on the job."

"Yeah, that would've been…awkward."

"To say the least."

Not that the past few minutes hadn't been even remotely awkward. At least she knew, and they could move forward as professionals. But he couldn't help feeling disappointed.

2

"Hailey!" Ray called as he strode toward her inside King Station.

Hailey turned toward Michael. "Do you have a minute? I'd like to introduce you to my brother." Maybe it was a stall tactic, but she wanted them to meet nonetheless. She released her hold on her two bags when Ray reached her.

"Hey, there." Ray held out his hand to Michael. "I'm Ray, Hailey's brother."

"Michael. Co-owner of MM Enterprises."

Ray's eyes widened slightly. "It's great to meet you. I didn't realize you'd be traveling together."

"It was a surprise to us too." Michael shifted the duffel bag strap on his shoulder. "My ride should be here any minute. It was nice meeting you. See you Monday, Hailey." He strode toward the exit at the other end of the train station.

Ray grinned. "It's good to have you home." He opened his arms. "May I have a hug?"

She stepped into his bear hug and gave him a quick squeeze before stepping back. Their family wasn't really the hugging type, but his wife must have rubbed off on him, or maybe it was his kids.

"Is this everything?" Ray reached for her two suitcases.

"I shipped the rest to your house. I hope you don't mind."

"Not at all. When do you expect it?"

"Hopefully by Friday. Are you alone?"

"Yes. Katie is with the little ones at home, and Emily has school today."

"It's hard to imagine Emily going to school. I know I saw her at Christmas, but I still picture her as a little girl." She walked beside him through the exit and into the parking lot beside the station.

"She's still a little girl, just not a preschooler."

"How has she adjusted?"

"Very well. Katie and I are quite pleased, and Emily loves her cousins." Ray stopped beside a large black SUV. He popped open the back and placed her luggage inside. "Katie is looking forward to having you around."

"Really?" She hopped into the front seat.

Ray buckled in. "Why do you sound so surprised?"

"We're not close. You kept her a secret from the family, and then I went away to school." She shrugged. "Things were so weird then."

"We were all in a different place after Renee and Matt died, but things are better now."

"I agree." She bit her bottom lip. She hadn't told

their mom she was coming home. "Did you mention anything to Mom about me?"

"You asked me not to."

"Thanks." Relief filled her. She could only deal with one branch of her family at a time.

"I assumed you planned to surprise her. Have you forgotten how much she hates surprises?"

"Actually, I did forget." But surely this kind of surprise would be okay.

"Tell me about your new job."

Her heart skipped a beat at the image her brother's question brought to mind. She'd been attracted to Michael since the moment they'd met, but he made it clear there was no fraternizing with his employees. "I know the gist of what I'm doing, but not the details. The idea is for me to guide the company in the right direction as they expand. We don't want to grow too fast or too slow."

"According to Ian, they've been growing really fast."

"Yes, and that worries me. Growth is good, but not if they can't support that growth internally."

Ray nodded.

"Speaking of growth. How is your athletic club doing? You mentioned wanting to open a branch on the East side. Did that ever happen?"

"I'm actually looking into the possibility. Tasha's been pushing me to expand for a long time."

"She's still working for you? Somehow I thought she would've moved on by now."

"Nope. She is an asset to The Ring. I'd hate to lose

her, especially with her background as a physical trainer, front desk manager, and her recently acquired Masters in Business Management. She's a triple threat. I'm seriously considering asking her to manage the East side location if it actually happens."

"Wow. Good for her. I hadn't heard she'd gone back to school."

Ray pulled into his driveway. "The kids are a little shy, but they'll warm up to you in no time."

Butterflies filled Hailey's stomach. "Thanks for the warning. I have gifts for them in one of my suitcases. Is it okay?"

"Absolutely. What'd you get them?"

"Chicago Cubs stuffed animals. I figured they're still young enough to enjoy those."

"Yep. But you know we're all Mariners fans here."

She chuckled. "I know. But hey, I was in Chicago." She got out and waited while her brother retrieved her luggage.

"Katie has the garage apartment ready for you."

"You don't have a tenant?"

"No. We had a student living there last year, but we never got around to finding a new renter. When we heard you were moving back, Katie went into a cleaning and decorating frenzy. I hope you like it."

"That was sweet of her."

"We thought you'd be more comfortable in your own space. If it's to your liking, we can work out a rental agreement."

This was turning out better than she'd dreamed.

"Thanks!" She knew Ray would give her a great deal. She'd imagined living downtown in the heart of everything, but living here would save her a lot of money.

"Let's get your bags upstairs. You lead." Ray hoisted one suitcase in each hand and climbed the stairs that ran along the outside of his garage to the apartment above.

Hailey pushed the door open, somewhat shocked it was unlocked.

"Surprise!" Several voices shouted.

Hailey jumped then laughed. Her sister-in-law, nieces, and nephew stood clustered under a banner that read, "Welcome home, Hailey."

"Thank you! I can't believe you did all of this. I heard you were at school, Emily."

"Aunt Katie picked me up early, so I could be here when you arrived."

Katie rubbed a hand up and down Emily's back. "We wanted you to know how happy we are that you're home and how proud we all are of you." She motioned toward her son who was bouncing up and down in place. "And in case you haven't figured it out yet, the kids are looking forward to having their Aunt Hailey around."

She looked to the children and smiled. "I've missed the three of you." She opened her arms wide and Emily rushed to her. Hailey didn't hold it against the younger ones for not joining their cousin. In all fairness, little Sophie didn't really know her. She was only eighteen months old and wouldn't remember her from this past Christmas. Alex was three, and he likely had no memory of her either.

"Aunt Katie said you're going to live here." Emily released her hold on Hailey's waist.

"I am, for a while at least." She really wanted to make it on her own and not be dependent on her brother's charity, but she appreciated the helping hand right now.

"Good." Emily grabbed her arm and pulled her toward the rest of the family who watched quietly. "This is Alex. He's in his terrible threes."

"Am not," her nephew declared with hands at his waist.

Hailey chuckled. "Good for you, Alex. No nephew of mine could possibly be terrible."

Katie swung Sophie into her arms. "Sophie has been talking non-stop about her auntie." She looked to her daughter. "This is Auntie Hailey. Can you say hi?"

Sophie tucked her head below Katie's chin and nuzzled into her neck. "Hi," Sophie whispered.

Her niece was adorable. "Hi, sweetie."

Ray cleared his throat. "How about you get settled, then meet us in the kitchen for a late lunch in about an hour?"

"Okay. Thanks." Her family scampered out and sounded like a herd of cattle tromping down the stairs that ran outside her apartment. She stood in the middle of the studio loft. "Home sweet home." She turned slowly. The queen-size bed with a simple white duvet against the far wall called to her. After the long ride from Chicago she looked forward to seeing if it was as cozy as it looked. The kitchenette at the opposite end of the space appeared adequate, but the tiny living space Katie had arranged for her was quite a step up from when Katie had lived here. The light blue sofa rested atop a faded, but clearly new cream and light blue rug, which she loved. How had her sister-in-law known exactly what she'd like, right down to the low-profile chairs in a blue damask fabric that faced the couch, completing the living space?

She'd have to thank Katie and Ray later for thinking of her tastes, but right now she needed to unpack. Too bad there wasn't a walk-in closet, but the armoire/wardrobe would have to suffice. She quickly hung the two new suits she'd purchased in Chicago after landing her job, then added the rest, almost all of which was more suited to a college coed than a professional office. She'd definitely need to shop once she got her first paycheck.

She glanced at her watch—enough time to check messages before joining everyone in the main house. She sat on the closest chair. "Mm...this is nice." She shot off a text to her best friend from high school. They'd kept in touch through the years, and she hoped to reconnect with Paige Graham.

Her phone rang. She checked the screen and smiled. "Hey, there."

"You're finally back," Paige said. "We need a girls' night. How'd it go with the hunk from the train?"

Hailey chuckled. "A girls' night sounds wonderful. My brother set me up in his garage apartment. You'll have to come over, and we'll have popcorn and watch a movie."

"Name the day and time, and I'm there."

"Tomorrow at six. I'll throw together a light dinner for us."

"I can't wait. And don't think for a second I didn't notice how you sidestepped talking about Mr. Train Hunk."

"I'll tell you that story tomorrow. I need to get downstairs. My brother and his family are expecting me for a late lunch."

"Okay. See you tomorrow."

Hailey pocketed her phone. Coming home was the right thing to do, but somehow she needed to get the courage to deal with her mom. That task wouldn't keep.

3

"I'm so glad you're home to stay." Paige tossed a piece of popcorn into her mouth.

"Thanks." Hailey carried two tall glasses of soda to the couch where her friend had made herself at home then sat.

"I sense a but. What's wrong?"

"Nothing's wrong. It's just I haven't told my mom that I'm back in Seattle."

"Why not?" Genuine curiosity rested on Paige's face.

"You know how she was when I left and how standoffish she's been. Mom can hold a grudge like a pro."

"Mmm. But won't she get over it since you're home to stay?"

"I don't know. Maybe. I suppose it depends on if it will benefit her in some way. I love her, but Mom is self-centered and has a ridiculous sense of entitlement."

"Do you regret leaving?"

"Not for a second. I needed to be on my own. I don't think I'd have been hired by MM Enterprises if I hadn't struck out on my own. Living in Chicago gave me the confidence I need to do my job."

Paige studied her for a moment. "You do seem different."

Hailey chuckled. "It's called maturity and getting out from under my mother's constant involvement in my life. She was so mad at me when I left that she never even called me. I always had to be the one to reach out. Which I didn't do more than once a month." She kicked off her sneakers and got more comfortable. "It's like I can finally breathe and be who I was meant to be."

"Sounds freeing." Paige frowned.

"What's wrong?"

"I'm beginning to regret not going away like you did. You make it sound so amazing." Her face turned a soft shade of pink. "I admire the choice you made and look at you now. You have your own apartment, while I still live with my parents."

"I'm not exactly on my own. My brother is helping me out until I can manage everything by myself."

"And you will. I'm so proud of you."

"Don't be too proud. I still have to tell her I'm in Seattle and navigate her drama. I'm not looking forward to it, either." Her stomach had been in knots for days, knowing what was likely headed her way. Mom could make the evil step-mother in all the movies look not so bad.

"I don't blame you. Maybe you should take Ray with

you when you go to see her."

"Good idea." Hailey reached for the remote. "Are you sure you want to watch a movie? We could visit instead and give each other manicures." She held out her hand with one chipped nail.

Paige gasped. "Don't you start your new job on Monday?"

Hailey nodded.

"You're in serious need of a mani. Go get your stuff. I'll do your nails. I just had mine done yesterday." Paige wiggled her fingers.

"I love that shade of pink. I'm going to skip the polish though." She hopped up and dug through her purse. She always had manicure stuff close at hand. "Here you go." She sat on the floor on the other side of the coffee table from her friend and held out her hand with the chipped nail.

"When you were on the train you told me about a guy. What was his name again? Sorry, he's train-hunk man in my head." She snickered.

"Michael."

Her face brightened. "Right. Did you get his number?"

"You could say that. Turns out he's the co-owner of MM Enterprises."

"No." Her mouth hung open for a second.

"Yes. And he made it abundantly clear that there will be no fraternizing."

"Pooh."

Hailey laughed. "I've missed you." She needed this

night with her friend more than she'd realized. "Anything new in your life?"

Her friend's brow scrunched. "I wish. I'm working full time now."

"That's new. Why didn't you say so sooner? Where?"

"I'm working for a harbor boat tour company on the Sound. It's actually fun since I do several things. We rotate so no one has the same job all the time. Sometimes I'm a deckhand and other times the tour guide. There's more, but being a tour guide is my favorite."

"Fun. How'd you get the job?"

"You know how much I like being on the water, and well, I was down on the pier one day and it hit me that I should apply. It's seasonal, but it's such a great experience. Maybe once the season ends, I'll try to get a job at the aquarium. My parents are upset because I'm not working for NOAA."

"They expect you to use your marine biology degree."

"Yeah, but there are other ways to put my knowledge to good use. I plan to apply at the aquarium soon."

"Great idea. You know...I'm used to having a roommate. And I'm not sure I'll like living alone. You interested in rooming with me?"

"Ah...Yeah! When can I move in?" She looked around the studio and frowned. "Uh, there's no room for a second bed."

Hailey laughed. "Let me figure some things out first. Ray offered to rent me this place, but I really wanted to live in the heart of the city. It'd be much more doable with a roommate."

Paige squealed then slapped her hand over her mouth. "Sorry. I hope they didn't hear in the house."

"Not likely."

A minute later pounding sounded on her door.

"Then again…" Hailey went to the door and looked out. "It's Ray." She pulled open the door.

"I heard a scream."

"How?"

"The kitchen window is open and you left your window open too."

She glanced toward the window. "Right. I forgot. We're fine. Sorry to alarm you. But as long as you're here, do you think you could take me to see Mom tomorrow?"

"I play one on one basketball with Ian first thing, but I could be ready to go by ten. Does that work for you?"

"Sounds perfect. Thanks."

He nodded. "Hi, Paige."

She waved from her position on the couch. "Long time no see, Ray. Sorry for the false alarm. I got a little excited."

He chuckled. "Good night, girls. See you in the morning, Hailey."

She locked the door, then slid the window closed. Her carefree mood from earlier vanished—she would see her mother in the morning as well.

Hailey took a deep breath and pressed the doorbell to her childhood home. Birds tweeted from a nearby tree branch, oblivious to the storm that was about to come in the form of her mother.

"I don't hear anything. Do you think she's not home?" She tilted her head toward Ray.

"Wishful thinking. She's usually here this time of day. Maybe she's out back gardening." He pulled a key ring from his pocket and let them in.

Hailey followed her brother inside and paused in the entryway. Not much had changed, except for the closed-up smell. Had her mother become a recluse? And what was up with the gardening? Mom hated to get her hands dirty.

Ray strode to the French doors that led to the large backyard. Sure enough, her mother sat on her knees hunched over a flowerbed that already looked impeccable.

"Hi, Mom. Look who's home!" Ray slipped his arm across Hailey's shoulders. "Stop being a chicken," he whispered out of the side of his mouth.

Their mom stood, brushing off her gloved hands. She slid them off one finger at a time, clearly in no hurry. "You could have called. I would have prepared brunch for us."

The sour tone in her mother's voice sent the message loud and clear. Hailey would not be welcomed back with open arms.

"I wanted to surprise you." Hailey opened her arms. "Surprise." She grinned.

"How long are you staying?"

Hailey glanced to her brother as her arms fell to her side. "I've actually moved back to Seattle."

Mom's face brightened for only a second then the same dour look took over—typical. "I suppose you need a place to stay. I repurposed your old room, but you can stay in the guest room. The stuff you left behind is either in boxes in the basement or donated to charity."

"You donated my stuff?" Her pulse jumped and warmth rushed through her. How dare she dispose of her belongings?

"I know that look, and before you say something you'll regret, I only got rid of stuff I knew you wouldn't want. When will you be moving back in?"

Ray's arm left her shoulders, leaving her feeling exposed. "Her housing is covered."

Shock blipped across Mom's face before being replaced with a cool look. "Good." She slipped her gloves back on then squatted onto the kneepad. "Next time call before you come. I'm busy. Ray, help your sister with her boxes. If they're still here when I'm done, I'll assume you no longer want them, and they will be donated as well."

Hailey clenched and unclenched her hands. Her throat thickened—it seemed time had done nothing to improve her mother's attitude. Mom enjoyed playing the victim.

"We'll be sure to do that. Thanks for the warm welcome." She turned and left without looking back. She marched down to the basement and noted a small contingent of boxes in the corner. "That must be my stuff."

Ray rested a hand on her shoulder. "You okay?"

She took a shaky breath. "Not really. Let's just grab my stuff and go." She hoisted a box into her arms. "Will you put another light one on top?"

"Sure." He placed a second box in such a way that she could see over the top. "I'll grab these last two and meet you at my rig."

Hailey stomped up the stairs and out the door, depositing the boxes at Ray's vehicle. She'd been foolish to think Mom would behave the way her friends' moms did. Victoria O'Brien had never been a conventional mother, and clearly she never would be.

Ray opened the back of the SUV and placed the boxes inside. "I'm sure glad Katie took the stroller out the last time she drove this."

"Mmm." Hailey climbed into the passenger seat.

Ray slid in beside her and placed a hand on her knee. "You're shaking the entire vehicle."

"I didn't realize I was bouncing my knee."

He pulled out of the driveway and headed toward home. "I'm sorry about how things went down. I'd really hoped for a more positive outcome."

"Me too. I guess me not living with her cemented

it."

"Sounded like it to me too."

She looked at her brother. "I'm twenty-four. I should be able to live on my own without feeling like I'm being a terrible daughter."

"I agree. Mom was never the same after the accident."

"I know. That's why I left, but I'd really hoped things had improved."

"You and Katie both. Mom is civil to her most of the time, but her disdain for my wife is never too far beneath the surface. Thankfully the kids haven't picked up on it."

"Yet." Once her nieces and nephew were older, they were sure to notice the dark side of their grandmother.

"I know I already said it, but I'm really sorry she was so cold toward you."

"Nothing less than I should have expected." Their mom was exceptional at giving the cold shoulder. It was a wonder she had any friends, considering how easily offended she was.

"Yeah. Same here. But still, I'd hoped she'd try to be nice."

She looked in his direction. "You do know our mom, right?"

Ray chuckled. "Point taken." He glanced her way. "You did the right thing coming today, regardless of the reception."

"I know, but it still stings. I wish for once she wouldn't play the victim card and see things from my point of view. "

They rode back to Ray's house in silence. He parked in the driveway. "Will you be joining us for dinner tonight?"

"No thanks. I have some stuff I need to do." She got out of the car and trudged up the stairs before she lost control of her emotions. She was used to their mom being self-absorbed, but her heart still hurt.

4

Early Monday morning Michael sat across from his business partner, Mason Gellar, in his office at MM Enterprises.

Mason tapped his desk with a pencil. "I don't have to tell you I'm uneasy about bringing in an economist as head of our business development. Hailey is competent, and her references are top notch, but what if we're sinking all this money into a new position only to have her steer us wrong?"

Michael steepled his fingers. His elbows rested on his desk. "We talked about this before I went to Chicago to interview her. That was the entire reason I did the interview in person. If you were uneasy, why didn't you say something before I hired her?"

"I'm not uneasy about her per se, but rather about the idea of taking on an expensive employee."

Michael shook his head. "She's young, enthusiastic, and has an air of confidence that her record supports. She's going to do great here, and in the process, she'll more than make up for what she's costing us."

"Maybe we can make it a contract job."

Michael shook his head. "Too late. That should have been worked out in the interview. I must stick by my word."

"Good point and I agree, but I don't know how to ease my worry any other way."

"I'm sorry you feel this way. Reality is, she might cost us more as an employee, but it's a moot issue." Michael stretched out his long legs and sighed. "She's supposed to be in my office first thing this morning. Please be there too." What was going on with Mason? His cousin wasn't usually such a worrywart.

He stood and headed down the short hallway to his office where he spotted Hailey looking lost near the unoccupied reception desk. She wore a professional-style skirt and blazer. A little blah compared to what he'd seen her in before, but she dressed for the role well. Her long hair was pulled up into a bun. He much preferred it down but didn't dare say so.

Hailey looked his way and raised her hand. "Good morning. I guess I'm a little early."

He grinned. "You'll fit right in." He motioned for her to follow. "Mason will be joining us shortly, and the rest of the staff will arrive by eight. Your office is this way."

"I get an office?"

"Considering your role in this company, I think that would be best. Don't you?"

"Yeah...I mean yes." She quickly walked over to

him. "Sorry. I'm a little nervous. I probably shouldn't have said that."

He chuckled. "Relax, Hailey. If it'll make you feel better, there's an unopened bag of chocolate-covered almonds in the top drawer of your desk."

She grinned. "That was nice. Thanks."

He nodded. "Sure. But, you have nothing to worry about." Unless her skills didn't live up to her reputation. Then they were all in trouble.

"If you say so." She took a deep breath then blew it out between her lips.

"Feel better?"

She grinned. "Nope. Think I'll go tear into that candy."

He chuckled. He could see why people liked her. She wasn't afraid to show her feelings. That could be both positive and negative in the business world. Hopefully, she'd rein it in when inappropriate. He stopped at the door to her office. "This is it. If you need anything, please let Thomas, our office manager know. He'll be by at eight to get you logged into the computer network."

"You have a male office manager?"

"Is that a problem?"

"No. It surprised me. I've only known female office managers. It's not a problem."

"Good. My office is across the hall and Mason's was the first one we passed." He should've stopped and introduced her. No matter, Mason would meet her soon. "Once you're settled, come to my office. We have a lot to go over."

She nodded then turned and went into her space at the same time he turned and went into his. He sat behind his desk, which gave him a direct view into her office. What would she do? She only had a briefcase-like purse with her.

She went straight to her desk and pulled open the top drawer. A second later she poured her vice into her hand and tossed them into her mouth. At least she was predictable, and there were worse things she could eat than chocolate-covered almonds.

Hailey crunched on the chocolate treat. Michael would be a good boss, especially if he kept her stocked in chocolate-covered almonds. Time to get down to business.

She'd studied up on MM Enterprises and felt ready to get to work. The short hand on the clock clicked to the eight. Time to meet the other half of MM. She stood and walked across the hall.

A dark-haired man sat in the chair facing Michael. He turned when she tapped on the doorjamb. His neatly trimmed beard and sparkling brown eyes drew her like a bear to honey. *Ack*. She couldn't be attracted to both of her bosses. She needed to get it together.

Michael motioned her to enter. "Hailey, this is Mason, my business partner."

Mason stood. He dwarfed them both. He was linebacker large.

"You don't happen to play pro-football on the side?" She chuckled. Her nerves were getting the best of her again. She needed to zip it.

Mason slid a look to Michael. "I played in college. It's nice to meet you, Hailey. Michael and Ian have both sung your praises."

"I hope I can live up to your expectations." She sobered—note to self—Mason is sensitive about his size.

"Time will tell. Have a seat." Mason motioned toward the chair beside his.

She tried to ignore the rapidly growing butterfly colony in her stomach.

"I trust you've had time to look over our business plan as well as our prospectus."

"I have. Your company is solid, but I've noted a few areas that could be strengthened." For the next hour they talked, exchanging ideas and setting up a short term and long term plan for her.

Mason stood. "It seems you're already proving your worth, Hailey. Welcome to MM Enterprises." He looked at Michael. "Did she sign her contract yet?"

Michael shook his head and handed Hailey an envelope. "I meant to give this to you when you came in this morning, so you could look it over and ask questions when we were all together. Before you do anything else, please spend some time reading it over. I'll need it signed before you go to lunch."

She grasped the envelope, gave each man a polite

smile and did her best to walk, not run to her office. With shaky legs, she sat behind her desk. She could do this. The meeting went well, her bosses seemed impressed—then why was she so nervous?

The envelope.

She pulled out the contents, and starting from the top of page one read the five-page document word for word. Basically, she was committing to this company for the next year. Everything was written in their favor. If she messed up, they could fire her and she'd have no recourse, plus she had to sign a non-disclosure agreement. As if she'd work for their competitors while employed here anyway, but the clause stating she couldn't work for their competitors if she was fired had to go.

She stood and walked across the hall to Michael's office. "You have a minute?"

"Of course. Take a seat."

She sat. "I can't sign the contract as written."

A frown marred his handsome face. "What part is causing a problem?"

"The section that says if I'm fired I can't work for any of your competitors for six months. That's not fair. You'd cut off my livelihood."

He nodded and held out his hand. "May I?"

She handed over the document.

He took a red pen and crossed that section out then signed beside the spot. "Get Mason to sign off too, and you will need to initial it as well."

"That's it? No discussion or debate?" That was too

easy.

"Our lawyer put that in there. I thought it was a bit much for a financial advisor. It's not like you are creating software for us." He shrugged. "I trusted her, and went with it. I don't want to lose you over that. Besides, after what I heard from you today, firing you won't be an issue."

"Okay. Thanks." She took the contract and headed for Mason's office. That went much better than she'd expected. She rapped on Mason's door. "Excuse me. Michael said to have you sign off on this." She handed him the contract and pointed to the spot in question.

With barely a cursory glance, he signed it and handed it back. "Glad to have you onboard, Hailey." His phone rang. "Excuse me."

She walked out of the office and spotted Ian. She strolled over to him. "Hey, there."

"You're here! Ray didn't say how the interview went. Congratulations."

"Thanks."

"Are you settled in?"

"Pretty much. Thanks for recommending me for this job."

"You deserved it. You'll enjoy working here. The M's are great to work for."

She chuckled. "You call them the M's?"

"Everyone does." He lowered his voice. "But not to their faces."

"Got it. I better get to work." She headed to her office and closed the door. From her position at her desk, she could see through the glass walls to Michael's office across the hall. He was talking on the phone. Maybe she should move her desk so he wouldn't be such a distraction.

Michael looked up and met her gaze. She sucked in a breath and focused on her computer screen. First thing tomorrow she'd see about rearranging this space.

At five o'clock, she powered off her computer, packed up, and headed out. Michael and Mason stood near the reception desk, talking animatedly to the receptionist. Hailey slunk past them, hoping to go unnoticed.

"Hailey," Michael's baritone rang out. "Hold up a minute."

She stopped and faced the small group. "Yes?"

"We need two women on our company co-ed softball team. Savannah is in, so that leaves you."

Hailey looked around the bullpen, and for the first time realized there was only one other woman besides her and Savannah. "Umm...I don't know."

"We need you," Mason said. "Without you we'll be disqualified."

"What did you do before I got here?"

Savannah shot her an impatient look. "Bree quit last week."

Michael frowned. "And she was our best batter."

Hailey's mouth had grown dry. She wasn't an athlete. Sure, she held her own in PE class, but she didn't play sports. Did she even know how to hold a bat properly? "If I'm not on the team, there is no team?"

Mason nodded.

"I have a friend who loves softball. If I get her onboard, could she do it instead?"

"Good question." Michael pulled his phone out. "It says here that if enough women are not available within the company then we may substitute."

"Whew. Then count me out. I'll talk to my friend." Surely Paige would be willing to join their team.

"In that case, count me out too," Savannah said. "I thought this was a requirement. But if she's not playing then neither am I."

Mason and Michael sighed in tandem.

Hailey felt like joining their sigh-fest. Good grief. "Fine. I'll play, but I'm warning you, I'm not great."

"Yes!" Mason pumped his fist. "You back in, Savannah?"

"Sorry. I'm out."

"But you're already on the roster. And we have a jersey with your name on it."

"Not my problem."

Hailey sashayed over to Savannah. "You know, we girls need to stick together."

The men had worried looks on their faces.

"What do you mean?" Savannah asked.

"Only that if you're not on the team then I don't get to be either. I know we work in the same office, but we're all so busy, warming the bench together could be fun."

"Except they actually make us play."

Hailey wrinkled her nose. "How rude." She shot a

playful look toward the men. "Then I really need you there to show me the ropes. I'll see if I can get my friend to come along too. It'll be fun."

Savannah shrugged. "I guess it could be. Fine. I'll come to the next game, but no promises beyond that."

Hailey smiled. "Good enough for now. See you tomorrow." She headed for the elevator.

The whoosh of someone walking close behind made her look over her shoulder. "Hey, Michael."

"You were great back there with Savannah. Thanks."

"Sure."

"How was your first day?" He pressed the button to call the elevator.

"Fine. I'd like to move my desk around. Is that a problem?"

"I don't see why it would be. But I'm curious as to why?"

"I'm easily distracted. I'd like to put my back to the hall wall."

He nodded. "I see. You sure you don't want to give yourself a chance to get used to having people walk past your view all day? I imagine it won't be such a distraction after a while."

The doors opened, and they stepped inside the empty space. "I suppose I could wait a week and see how it goes."

"It's up to you. But waiting a week sounds like a good idea." He grinned. "I'm glad you joined our team. It'll be fun."

"Even if I can't hit the ball?" She watched for his reaction.

Surprise then disappointment crossed his face before he schooled it to be impassive. "We play to have fun, not to win."

"Liar." She giggled as the door opened, and a couple of people walked in.

Light rain splattered around Hailey as she stood on Pier 54 facing the water. A seagull landed on a railing and stared at her. "Sorry, fella. I don't feed birds. That's what the Sound is for." Her stomach rumbled. She felt for the bird but knew better than to feed him. There were signs posted saying not to because they created a huge mess on the Wharf.

She checked her watch for the second time in five minutes. Paige was late, and they had reservations nearby for dinner. Hopefully, she wouldn't be too much longer.

"Hailey!"

She whirled around at the sound of Paige's voice and waved to her friend who was rushing toward her. Hailey moved to meet Paige halfway. "There you are. How was work?"

"Busy. Sorry I'm late." She tucked her arm through Hailey's as they strolled toward their favorite seafood restaurant. "More importantly, how was your first day?"

"Interesting, exhausting, exhilarating…."

Paige chuckled. "Sounds well balanced." They entered the restaurant.

Paige gave her name to the hostess, who asked them to follow her. They were seated beside a window that looked out over the water.

Hailey relaxed into the chair. "This is perfect."

"Good. I knew you'd need this after your first day and requested a window seat."

"You're the best friend ever." She meant it too. Sure, she'd made friends while in Chicago and some might even become lifelong friends, but Paige already qualified as a lifelong friend and knew her better than anyone.

The waiter came and took their orders then moved on to another table.

"I need to ask you something before I forget. MM Enterprises has a softball team, and they are required to have at least two women on the team. I was hoping you'd agree to be an alternate. One of my co-workers is a little wishy-washy, and I'm afraid she might not show."

"It sounds like fun, but you don't play. How's that going to work?"

"I know how to play. I just don't." At least she'd played a little back in high school P.E. so she wasn't completely clueless.

"Do you even own a glove?" Paige looked at her with a raised brow.

"You know I don't." Hailey frowned. "I didn't think of that."

"Yes, but lucky for you, I still have my old one.

You're welcome to use it."

"One hurdle jumped. Will you play catch with me a couple of nights this week? I don't want to make a fool out of myself." Especially in front of Michael. He might be her boss and as such off limits, but she still wanted to impress him.

"Sure. Let's meet in a park so you can work on fielding too."

"What did I get myself into?"

"Nothing you can't handle, I promise. You were always athletic in high school, so I'm sure you'll be able to hold your own after some practice."

"The first game is Saturday. Somehow I don't think a couple hours of practice is going to make much difference."

"You'd be surprised. But if you're worried, why not plan to meet every night this week? The weather is supposed to clear and be nice the rest of the week."

"Works for me. I don't have anything better to do." Unless apartment hunting and daydreaming about her boss counted.

Off in the distance a ferry crossed the Sound. "How was work?"

"Busy, but fun. I really like what I'm doing. How about you? Do you think you're going to like your job?"

"I do. For the most part I like the people there. The owners are pretty cool and are clear about their expectations, so that's nice."

"Good."

Their fish and chips arrived and they dug in, eating

in comfortable silence. As much as Hailey liked her new job, she didn't want it to become her life. She saw firsthand what that had done to her brother and other members of their family. She wanted balance, which meant dinner out with friends, softball games—though technically work—church, and spending time with her adorable nieces and nephew.

Hailey wiped her greasy fingers on a napkin and released a sigh of contentment. "Thanks for suggesting this."

"Sure. I hate to eat and run, but I'm helping my mom make strawberry jam tonight."

"You're going to have a late night."

"My mom's always been a night owl, and I have tomorrow off so I can sleep in." They placed cash on the table for their bill and tip then left. "Would you like a ride?"

"I'll catch the bus." Hailey hugged Paige then strolled to the bus stop. Happiness bubbled inside her. It was good to be home, and one way or another she'd find a way to fix things with her mom.

5

Tuesday evening Michael jogged through his neighborhood park. He preferred to take an early run in the morning during the summer months, but today had been hectic thanks to a power outage.

Two women were playing catch across from the covered picnic area. One looked familiar. *Hailey?* He slowed to confirm his suspicion. Sure enough, it was. She barely caught the ball. He winced at her horrible form. She was fortunate she hadn't hurt herself. She tossed the ball back to her friend.

"You got lucky on that one, Hailey. Next time get under the ball and hold your glove like this." Her friend knew what she was talking about. Could this be the woman Hailey had mentioned?

He slowed to a walk and approached the women. "Hi, there."

Hailey turned her head in his direction right as the ball smacked her in the chest. She cried out and hugged her arms to her chest.

"Sorry for my bad timing. I didn't mean to distract you." He jogged over to her and rested a hand on her shoulder. "Are you okay?"

Her friend rushed up to them. She shot a warning look at him. "Hands off!"

He raised his hand and stepped back. "Hailey and I work together."

Her face relaxed. "Oh. Sorry for shouting at you. Hailey, are you okay? I didn't realize you weren't looking."

"I'll be fine. You surprised me."

"I noticed."

"It's fine. I learned a lesson. Never take your eye off the ball."

Her friend chuckled. "Took you long enough to figure that out." She held her hand out to Michael. "I'm Paige. And you are?"

"Michael. I'm Hailey's boss."

"Oh."

Oh? What was that supposed to mean? He shrugged off the implied slight. "Are you the friend that might be joining our softball team?"

"That would be me. I play third."

"That's my base too. Do you have experience in any other positions?"

"Not really. But I suppose you could put me in the outfield if you need me to play."

"We'll see. Thanks for agreeing to help us out."

"Sure." She looked to Hailey who had finally released her hold on her chest and appeared to be back to normal. "You ready to go?"

"Yeah. I've had enough for one night."

"You're practicing for Saturday?" Michael didn't expect that she'd go the extra mile for a softball game. The team had been having practice twice a week for the past month, but now that the games had begun they didn't have the time.

"That was the plan. It seems I don't know as much about catching a ball as I thought."

Paige frowned. "You'll get there. I promised that you'd be game-ready by Saturday and you will be. So long as handsome men don't keep distracting us." She grinned.

Michael's face heated. "I'll be on my way. See you." He took off at a slow jog. He knew Hailey was a go-getter, but if she didn't know how to play why had she agreed to be on the team? Probably because she'd been given little choice. He never should have assumed she played softball. Her athletic physique fooled him, but regardless the team needed her. He sure hoped she knew how to swing a bat since everyone on the roster was required to be in the batting lineup—a stupid rule their league had adopted this season.

Since Hailey had started at the office things had been going smoothly. Granted she'd only been there two days, but he had a good feeling about Hailey. He was certain his brother would approve of her as well.

Speaking of Trent, he needed to finish his run and get home. His brother had been in Europe for the better part of two weeks and should be home now. He'd finish his normal loop through the park and give Trent time to unpack. Who was he kidding? His brother lived out of a suitcase thanks to his job with MM Enterprises, but that's what he wanted so Michael wouldn't feel sorry for him.

He lengthened his stride and continued along the well-used path, passing joggers and walkers. He rounded the last bend then cut off to the left and headed toward home, a bungalow in an established neighborhood. He waved to his neighbor as he climbed the stairs to his front door.

The door swung open. He jumped back. "Trent. You surprised me."

"You knew I was coming home today." Trent stepped out of the way, allowing him to enter their cozy home.

"Are you on your way out?"

He held up a stack of mail. "Thought I'd read my mail out here on the porch. It's such a nice day."

"How was your trip?"

"Better than I expected. Go get cleaned up then we can grab a bite to eat."

"There's food in the fridge."

Trent made a face.

Michael chuckled as he took the stairs two at a time to his bathroom. Ten minutes later he pocketed his keys and wallet and headed out the door. "Fast enough for you?"

Trent looked up from an auto magazine, fatigue covering his face. "Too fast." He stood. "Be right back."

A moment later his brother returned and locked up the house. "Frank's Gyros?"

"Where else would we go on a sunny summer evening?" The food truck specialized in Greek food. The name didn't exactly fit the cuisine, but it never seemed to hurt business.

They walked the half-mile to the food trucks. "How was your trip?"

"Uneventful."

"Those are the best kind. How did the meeting go with our investors?"

"I sent you a report. Didn't you read it?"

"You know I hate reading those things. Mason looked it over."

Trent sighed.

Michael studied his twin's profile and noted a few more lines than the last time he'd been home. What was going on with his brother? Had all the travel finally caught up to him? That couldn't be it. For as long as he could remember Trent had the travel bug. That was one of the reasons he hired him. But if he wasn't travel weary what else could be wrong? He tucked away the concern for now, unwilling to deal with anything unpleasant so soon after his homecoming. "I took a trip of my own to Chicago to interview our new financial advisor and wonder-woman extraordinaire."

"You're kidding. Good for you. You finally found someone?"

"Yes, thanks to Ian's recommendation." They meandered into the parking lot where the food trucks gathered in the evenings and found their favorite eatery in its typical location. They each ordered their usual, a lamb gyro. Then took their food to a nearby picnic table shaded by a maple tree.

"So tell me about the new hire." Trent bit into his gyro.

"She's smart, witty, has a thing for chocolate-covered almonds, and she's a recent graduate with a degree in economics."

"How is it you know about her snack food?"

Michael explained about their train ride back to Seattle. "I had no idea she'd be on the same train as me." Had he known, he would have booked one for the following day and taken a day to sightsee in the Windy City. Still they'd bonded on their trip, and it had left him feeling like a heel for not correcting her during the interview when she'd made the wrong assumption.

His brother studied him.

"Knock it off."

"What? Just trying to get a feel on this situation."

"There is no situation. Hailey works for me. I don't fraternize with my employees."

"You fraternize with me."

"That's different, and you know it."

Trent shrugged. "Maybe, but if you're into her, you should ask her out."

"You of all people know better than to suggest that."

"So it didn't work out with Becky and me. That's how it goes." Trent shrugged off his yearlong relationship as though it'd been nothing, but he wasn't fooling Michael.

"We lost one of our best programmers when you dumped her." Trent had caught Becky out on a date with another man. Apparently she wasn't as serious as Trent and had only been using him, thinking he had the power to grow her career.

"I know, but look at the bright side. When she quit you found Ian. Not only is he a wiz, he's the one who recommended Hailey. Seems to me it all worked out in the end."

"How is it we're brothers?" Michael eyed his twin with dismay.

Trent took a bite and the sauce dripped down his chin. "Just goes to show even identical twins have their differences."

Michael grunted. "You almost done with that? It's been a long day."

"You're talking to me about long?" He stuffed the last bite into his mouth then stood.

Michael had half of his meal remaining and stayed seated.

"Aren't you coming? I thought you wanted to go."

He ignored the comment, knowing he had indicated exactly that, but only because he wanted to change the subject. He scarfed the rest of his sandwich in two bites. "Done. You must be dead on your feet. Isn't it the wee hours of the morning in London right now?"

"Yes and yes."

How his brother managed on little to no sleep, he'd

never know. He needed a full eight hours or he couldn't function. The best thing he'd ever done was hire his brother on as their bookkeeper and executive assistant to represent the company to clients as well as prospective clients. Trent actually enjoyed numbers and going to meetings, whereas he didn't—the perfect pairing. In reality his brother did so much more than what he was originally hired for. He was Michael's right-hand man and was sorely missed whenever he was gone for long stretches.

"Do we have a softball game this Saturday?" Trent asked.

"Yes. There will be a couple new players. While you were away Bree left the company."

"That's unfortunate, but she wasn't producing the way we'd hoped, so it's not a huge loss."

"I agree, which is why we aren't replacing her. But that left a hole on the team. Hailey is joining us and volunteered her friend if we're short. I don't think she trusts Savannah to show up." With good reason. He'd picked up on Savannah's attitude right away.

"I can't wait to meet Hailey. She's perceptive. Savannah hates playing softball." Trent climbed the stairs to their front porch.

"I'm going to sit out here for a while."

"Okay. I'll see you in the morning."

"Wait. You're going to the office?"

"You know I'll be there." Trent pulled open the screen door.

"Feel free to come in late."

"I might take you up on that. Good night." He went inside.

Michael could always count on his brother, which was why he'd hired him. He trusted no one more than Trent. He eased into the rocker their parents had given them as a house-warming gift when they bought the place two years ago. Dusk had set in. Crickets chirped and the faint sound of kids playing filled the otherwise quiet neighborhood.

His thoughts drifted to Hailey and her friend, practicing ball in the park. He couldn't help admiring her dedication. He needed more people like her in his life and business. So far it looked like he'd made the right decision in hiring her, but time would tell.

Hailey showered off the dust from the park then slipped into gray sweats and a pink T-shirt. She padded into her kitchenette and clicked on the electric teakettle for her evening cup of chamomile tea. She loved coffee during the day, but at night she was a tea girl.

A knock on her door drew her attention. She pulled it open. "Katie? Is everything okay?"

"Yes, I only wanted to come up and say hi. We haven't had much chance to talk since you returned."

"True. Come in. I was just boiling water for tea. Would you like a cup?"

Katie shook her head. "No thanks. I'm more of a hot chocolate kind of girl."

"I wish I had some to offer you. Ray said you used to work in a coffee shop."

"Yes. I love the scent but don't much care for the taste. There's a tin of hot chocolate in your cupboard, but I don't want any right now."

"Seriously?" She'd been so busy she hadn't noticed. "That was nice of you to stock it. Thanks."

"Sure." Katie moved to the couch and sat. "How are you settling in?"

"Pretty well, I think. I sure appreciate you and Ray letting me use this place until I can find my own."

"There's no rush. Ray likes having his little sister so close." She grinned and picked at a loose thread on the couch.

"I'm glad. But I want to be on my own. Somehow living above his garage doesn't feel very independent."

"I understand. How's the new job?"

"So far so good." The kettle clicked off, and she poured boiling water into a mug with a teabag, then took it back to the couch and sat. "It's only been a few days, but I think I'll like it there. My bosses are great, and I don't hate my co-workers."

Katie chuckled. "I'm glad. Brandi and I usually go to the company games to watch Ian play on Saturday. You're welcome to sit with us."

"That's sweet, but I'll be sitting with the team."

"Really?" Her voice hinted at surprise. "Your brother never mentioned you played softball."

"I don't. At least not well, but Paige is trying to help me so at the least I won't make a fool of myself."

"She sounds like a good friend. Is she the one who helped you with our wedding?"

Hailey nodded. "Paige and I have been besties forever."

"Sounds like me and Brandi."

"Exactly. I'm sure glad Ray and Ian are still close, even after our friends moved to England for a year."

"Me too," Hailey said. "If it wasn't for Ian, I wouldn't have this great job."

"Yeah. But just because someone leaves the country, it doesn't mean they won't be friends anymore. I'll admit it was rough when Brandi moved to England right after their wedding, but it was probably the best thing for both of us since we were all newlyweds. It allowed us to focus on our new relationships and bond to our spouses rather than having our close friendships distract us."

"I hadn't thought of that." There had always been something off about Ray and Katie's whirlwind wedding, and to this day she hadn't figured out what it was.

"I love your brother very much, but that wasn't always the case. Ray and I talked, and we both agree you deserve to know the truth."

"What are you talking about?"

"There was a reason we had a quickie wedding. Your brother was going to lose his business due to a clause in your grandfather's will stating he had to marry by his twenty-eighth birthday."

Hailey gasped. Her thoughts crashed into a pile of indecipherable rubble.

"Say something." Katie tucked a blonde strand of hair behind her ears.

"I don't know what to say. I can't comprehend a marriage like that. But you love each other now?" Her brother had never even hinted at the truth behind their marriage.

"Very much. I didn't realize it at the time, although I'd been in love with your brother for a long time before we married, but we were friends then and nothing more. When your sister and brother-in-law were killed in their car accident and left Emily an orphan, that set our course in motion."

"I wondered why the wedding was so last minute." If she hadn't been gripped with grief at the loss of her big sister, she might have thought to thoroughly question her brother, but instead she'd accepted his rushed marriage and went out of her way to help them pull it off.

"The biggest reason was we wanted Ian and Brandi to be there, and if we'd waited they would've already been in Europe."

"This is a lot to take in."

"I know. It was for me too when Ray told me about his situation. You know I was Emily's regular sitter and adored her, so it only made sense that I would become her nanny."

"I understand that part, but that's quite a leap to marriage."

"Yes, but God had His hand in it. We both felt like He was leading us to marry. We have no regrets. I love

Ray, and marrying him was the smartest thing I've ever done. Even if things were awkward and difficult at first."

"Wow." She shook her head. This was a lot to process, but it answered so many questions she'd had. "Why didn't Ray tell me and our mom?"

"He was protecting me. He wanted your mother to accept me as his wife and felt that if she thought he only married me as a means to an end she'd never respect me."

Hailey sighed. "He was probably right. How are you and my mom now? I know she was horrible to you before."

"She's...cordial."

Sadness enveloped Hailey. Why couldn't her mother see what a gem Katie was? "Thank you for trusting me with the truth. I know after all this time it would've been easier to ignore the past, and if you had, I would have been fine with it. But to be honest, I feel much closer to you now, knowing what you did for my family."

Katie's cheeks pinked. "I should go. Morning comes long before I'm ready most days." She stood.

Hailey set her untouched tea on the coffee table then walked with her sister-in-law to the door. "Good night, Katie."

"'Night."

Hailey locked up then clicked off the main lights, leaving on the low-watt bulb in the kitchenette. Katie had said the Lord had His hand in them marrying. She knew her brother was a strong Christian and apparently, so was Katie.

She sat back on the couch, tucked her knees to her chest, and stared into the semi-darkness. *Lord, it's pretty cool what you did for my brother. I could use Your hand in my life too.*

She'd never thought to ask Him about her relationships or pretty much about anything to do with her life. He was God. She had no doubt of His love, but surely He didn't have time for her and her problems. But if what Katie said was true, which she believed it was, then God did have time for people. She'd been raised in church and had been taught that He cared, but somehow bothering Him with things like everyday life seemed beneath Him. Did He really care about the little things as well as the big?

Did He have anything to do with her new job? And what did He think about her relationship with her mom? She shook her head. It was too late at night to be thinking this hard. She had an early morning and needed a clear head. Especially with how distracting Michael was proving to be, even with her desk resituated—she couldn't wait a full week to see how it went as Michael had suggested.

A text flashed on her phone.

Please meet me at the corner coffee shop at seven-thirty tomorrow morning. M

Michael? How odd. She continued reading.

Okay. Why?

We'll talk tomorrow.

How was she supposed to get a wink of sleep after a text like that?

6

Michael checked his watch for the third time in five minutes. He was early, but somehow thought Hailey would be as well. Businessmen and women bustled past him, seemingly oblivious to anything except their coffee fix. His caramel macchiato sat untouched on the bar in front of him as he faced the window looking out onto the sidewalk.

The door to the shop swung open, and Hailey rushed in. "I hope you weren't waiting long."

"Only a few minutes. I was early. I made a guess and ordered a chai tea latte for you."

She dipped her chin, and a small smile tilted her lips. "That was nice of you. Thanks. I'm a white mocha kind of girl, but I like these too. I took the bus so I couldn't get here any sooner."

"No problem. You're probably wondering why I asked you to meet me here before work."

She nodded.

"My brother, Trent, is back from his business trip to

Europe on behalf of MM. I wanted to get you up to speed on him because the two of you will be working closely together. He represents our company in all the foreign markets."

"Because you don't fly."

"Exactly, and schmoozing potential investors, clients, and board members is not Mason's strength."

"Okay. I'm curious why you don't fly?"

"It's not my thing."

"Nothing happened to make you afraid to fly?"

"Nothing traumatic." In an odd way he wished he did have a traumatic experience he could blame, but the idea of stepping foot in a huge tin can and allowing it to take him thousands of feet in the air where he had absolutely no control was more than he could fathom.

"All right then. What is your concern?" She pulled out her smartphone and opened her "notes" app.

He frowned. "You're taking notes?"

"This is a meeting, is it not? Therefore, I need to record what we talk about."

He reached for his coffee and took a long draw. He wasn't accustomed to this formal side of Hailey and much preferred the woman he met in Chicago last week. He placed the cup onto the bar. "As I stated, Trent manages our foreign accounts. When he's in the office, I want you to go through the latest data with him and determine if we're on the right track. Revenue has dropped in those markets recently, and I'd like to know why."

She sucked in the corner of her lip as she pecked the

screen with her thumbs. She glanced up at him. "What else?"

"That's it."

"Oh. I thought since we were here so early…"

"No. I like to be in the office early, so I had to adjust for that." He stood. "I'll see you there."

"Ah…okay."

He hesitated. "How's the practicing coming along?"

"You saw it last night. I wouldn't hold my breath that you have a new secret weapon." She stuffed her phone into her purse and stood. "Mind if I walk with you?"

"Actually, I don't want anyone to see us walking in together and get the wrong idea."

She frowned. "I didn't think of that. Perhaps meeting so early had to do more with your paranoia than beating the staff to the office." She raised a brow, grabbed her tea, then strutted from the shop.

He blew out a breath. "Well, that didn't go as expected." This was why he rarely hired women—he didn't know how to communicate well with them, and he felt socially awkward. He never should have said people would talk. With a sigh, he left.

Hailey closed the door to her office and dropped her bag beside her desk. She'd walked all the way around the block before coming to the office, giving herself time to cool off and think. Though she didn't appreciate what Michael had said, she had to respect that he was looking out for her too, not just himself.

Most of her classmates could only dream of landing a job like this one, and it stood to reason that some would be suspicious of the details surrounding her hiring.

She turned and glanced toward Michael's office—empty. She owed him an apology. For now, she had work to do. She wiggled the mouse and her computer screen came to life. After entering her passcode, she got to work.

A knock on her door drew her attention. Michael stood there, but he had changed clothes—odd. She waved him inside. "Hey, there. I'm glad you stopped by. I owe you an apology. I overreacted, and I'm sorry."

Michael held out his hand. "I'm Trent, Michael's twin brother."

Her heart skipped. She stood and shook his hand. "He didn't tell me you were twins. It's nice to meet you." Her face was overly warm. It would have been nice if Michael had mentioned that detail, but mix-ups probably happened often. "I was briefed earlier this morning about your work here."

"Should my ears be burning?" He grinned.

She laughed. "No. You're fine. Do you have a few minutes to tell me about your latest trip?"

"Everything is in my report, which I emailed to you right before knocking on your door."

She looked at the screen and nodded. Sure enough,

it came in while they were talking. "Excellent. If I have questions will you be available?"

"Sure. My office is right next door."

She'd noticed the empty space but hadn't given it a second thought with all she'd had to deal with this week.

"I wanted to stop in and welcome you to the company. It's a great place to work."

"Thanks. It seems like one big family."

He chuckled. "Cute."

"No pun intended."

He took a step back and leaned against the doorjamb. "I hear you'll be joining us at the company game on Saturday."

"You heard correctly. But I'm a beginner."

"Don't worry. You probably won't even need to play, other than to bat." He winked then left.

Charming was the first word that came to mind. Why couldn't Michael be like that? Then again, she'd thought the same of him when they'd first met. Hopefully, Trent wouldn't turn into a toad too.

Speaking of toads…she stood and crossed the hall. The door to Michael's office was open as usual, and he sat behind his desk lost in thought. "Can we talk?"

He looked up. "Of course. Take a seat."

She shook her head. "I'll be fast. I wanted to apologize for earlier."

"It's fine. I could've shown more finesse. I saw you met my brother."

"I did. You forgot to mention you're identical twins."

"Did I?" He raised a brow then turned his attention back to whatever he'd been working on when she'd come in.

She chuckled and left. He might be a toad from time to time, but the real man shone through when he let his guard down. Too bad he didn't do that more often. She liked that man.

The day flew by, and before it seemed possible, it was closing time. She quickly tidied up and headed for the elevator. Tonight was game night with her brother and his family. She couldn't wait. Hopefully, they would play a few games intended for people other than preschoolers. But if not, she'd always enjoyed a rousing game of Old Maid.

"Hailey, wait up."

She glanced over her shoulder. Trent speed-walked toward her. She stopped and waited until he reached her then kept on toward the elevator.

"What's your rush?"

"Family stuff. Did you need something?"

"We never connected over my report."

"Right. My day got away from me. How about we meet first thing in the morning?"

"Can't. I have a meeting in Portland."

"But you just returned from traveling."

"That's my purpose here. I'll be back on Friday. We can talk then. Will you write me into your schedule?"

"Of course. Have a safe trip." The elevator slid open, and she stepped in. Trent didn't. "You're not coming?"

"I have some stuff to finish up. See you Friday." He waved as the doors slid closed.

About an hour later, she knocked on Ray and Katie's kitchen door. She could see them through the window as they waved her in. The kitchen table was set up with finger food and a stack of games. "Hi. Thanks for including me in family game night."

Katie gave her a quick hug. "I'm glad you could make it. I was worried your job might keep you from being here."

"Actually, other than the softball game on Saturday, MM Enterprises respects business hours for the most part. Personally, I love that. My old job didn't, so this is a nice change."

"Good. Have a seat. The kids are washing their hands. As you can see, we are super casual on family night."

Ray pulled a homemade pizza, topped with veggies and cheese from the oven. "This smells amazing. I hope you don't mind that it's gluten free. We're so used to eating that way now, we don't notice the taste difference."

"It's fine. I almost forgot that Katie can't have gluten."

"I haven't forgotten." Katie said drily. "Life would be easier if I could, but I'm used to the extra work now, so I guess it's not such a big deal as it once was."

"At least you live in Seattle. There are lots of places to eat out with gluten-free options and even full menus. It's not like that everywhere."

"I've heard."

Her sister-in-law wasn't a traveler. Probably because she spent much of her growing up years in foster care, then married Ray young. When would she have had the time to travel? Ray certainly never went anywhere because of his athletic club.

"Aunt Hailey." Emily ran to her and gave her a hug. "I'm glad you came."

"Me too." Her insides warmed at the friendly reception. She wasn't sure how Emily would react to her. When she was a preschooler, she was sometimes shy with strangers. Granted she wasn't exactly a stranger, but her niece couldn't have many memories of their times together.

Her family, including the little ones, gathered at the table. Katie put Sophie in her highchair, and Alex climbed into a booster. Ray offered a blessing for the food then they dug in.

"How does this work? I see the games and the food are both out," Hailey said. "Doesn't that get a little messy?"

"It can." Ray cut up Alex's pizza. "Sophie is content to play with her food while we play games. Once the pizza is gone then we'll set up the first one."

She bit into the savory-smelling concoction and chewed thoughtfully. Though different than what she was accustomed to, it was still good.

After two hands of Old Maid and one round of Memory, the kids were done and headed to their bedrooms with Katie, leaving Hailey alone with Ray to wash dishes. She washed, and he dried.

"I spoke with Mom today."

"Oh?" Her good mood vanished.

"Yes. She invited us for brunch on Sunday."

"As in you and me? Or all of us?"

"You and me."

"Doesn't that bother you?" One would think their mother would want to spend time with her grandchildren, but they both knew Mom had never been a kid person.

"Not really. She's at least trying to reach out to you. It's a step in the right direction."

"I guess." She should be grateful, but all she felt right now was frustration. "Any reason why she talked to you rather than me?"

"I called her."

"Oh." She handed him the last pan. "I didn't think of that." She'd spent years avoiding any unnecessary conversations with her mother, and it had become a habit. One she needed to break if they were going to find healing—assuming her mom wanted that.

"Ian tells me you're fitting in well at work."

"Oh, yeah? I'm glad he thinks so. I like it there. I owe him for recommending me."

Ray draped the towel over the side of the counter. "Don't worry about it. Ian and I lost track of all the times we owed one another for this or that."

She laughed then sobered. "Katie told me about the circumstances surrounding your marriage."

"You mean when we first married?"

She nodded. "I wish you would've told me."

"It was better that you didn't know. It was a lot to deal with so soon after Renee and Matt's death. Plus, Mom would have made things impossible. As it was she was awful to Katie."

"Katie is a sweetie. It's hard to imagine anyone being mean to her, even Mom."

"Trust me, our mother has a tongue that cuts deep and wide, and she used it with abandon the day of our wedding."

Hailey winced. "I'm sorry. Katie didn't tell me."

"And she never will."

Hailey nodded. "You mind if I duck out?"

"Not at all. Thanks for joining us tonight. I know kid games aren't all that exciting."

"What? You mean you don't find it exhilarating to win at Memory? I personally consider it a great accomplishment."

He laughed. "Get out of here."

"So bossy." She left with a bounce in her step. Coming home had been the right thing to do.

7

Early Friday morning, Michael jogged beside Trent through their neighborhood. "How did the meeting in Portland go yesterday?"

"Not at all as I'd expected." His voice held an edge.

Michael glanced toward his brother. Trent generally let work wash off him like a waterfall cascading off boulders. "What's up?"

"What do you know about our potential client?"

"Little to nothing." Mason studied their clients to better understand how best to serve them, while Trent was the face of the company.

"Mrs. Morris believes family is important."

"Surprising, considering how successful her business is. I'd think she'd be married to her job."

"Complete opposite. In fact, I think half the staff is family, and held to high standards. Some are distant relatives but related nonetheless."

Michael rubbed a hand over his neck. "Okay. What am I missing? I thought the meeting yesterday was a formality and that the contract would be signed, sealed, and delivered." Somehow he didn't think that happened after all.

Trent frowned. "She sought us out because we were the only software development company with family at the helm that she liked. Somehow she learned that Mason is our cousin, and she likes that I take such a huge role in the company."

"That's great. So what's the problem?"

"She's bothered that there are no women in leadership. And suggested we appoint a female VP. Then said she was considering going with one of our competitors who had women in leadership roles."

"You're kidding?" Michael's pace slowed.

"I wish. She's playing games with us, and it infuriates me because we need her business."

His pulse picked up. "Who does she think she is? Pass on this contract. There'll be another one from someone who's not so manipulative. I don't want to work with a person like that."

Trent matched his slower pace. "Normally, I would agree, but we need this one. It's huge. On top of that, she might be right. A woman in leadership will add a dimension to the business we haven't explored. Women like working with other women. I think she could be onto something."

"Do you really think it's wise for me to allow her to dictate how I run the company? I sure don't."

"Here's the thing. We can't afford to brush off this deal. And she's not dictating anything. She simply made the comment about a woman VP then went on to inform me she was seriously considering another company as well. No threats, just conversation. I read into things a bit and feel like if we can provide female leadership here, she would choose us over our competition."

"She might not have come right out and said it, but her intent is clear. Why is this so important?" Michael slowed. What did Trent know that he didn't?

"Mason is gambling again, and it's bad this time. You could lose your business if we don't get the contract."

Michael stopped. "How did this happen?" Mason had been in counseling. Had he been lying to them? Well, clearly he'd been lying if he was gambling. It was too much. "Wait, what do you mean I could lose the business?"

Trent paced with hands resting on his hips only slightly winded. "I confronted Mason this week after I returned from Europe. He didn't want you to know he's been pilfering our profits to pay off his gambling debts."

Michael's chest squeezed. He started walking, to cool down from the run. "Why am I just now hearing this? If you knew when you returned, why not tell me then? Or why not clue me in to your suspicion before you left. Clearly you knew or at least suspected before you took off." He trusted Trent implicitly. How could he sit on this information for over three weeks?

"You're right. I discovered the discrepancy in the books right before my trip. My one day back in the office was spent sorting out the details and confronting Mason. I had hoped that this new contract would fix everything and spare you from having to know about it. Last time things were so rocky between the two of you, I thought it best to handle it myself."

"I can't believe this. I trusted him. I trusted you—I can't believe you didn't tell me as soon as you suspected something was wrong." At least now he understood the added lines to his brother's face and why he had seemed out of sorts.

"And you still can trust me. It's within the scope of my job to deal with this situation. I wanted to protect you, but I couldn't."

Trent was correct in saying it was his job to deal with Mason as well as the company finances, but at the same time this was huge and should have been brought to him. "Thank you for trying to protect me, but I don't need babying. I need the truth."

"I'm sorry. I did what I thought was best. What's done is done. Now we need to fix this."

"Agreed." Michael had been through this before with his cousin, but they'd caught what he was doing before he could do any real damage. Why hadn't he taken away Mason's ability to touch the company funds the first time this happened? "I can't believe I gave him a second chance."

"We both trusted Mason. You need to get him removed from all the company banking, so he can't get to the money anymore."

"I hate that it's come to this. I wanted to believe

he'd recovered from his gambling addiction." Michael stopped walking and looked at his brother. "Has he taken any more since you discovered what he was doing?"

"Thankfully, no. In fact, he's paid a little back, but not nearly enough."

"What am I going to do? I can't close the doors. So many people depend on MM Enterprises."

"Hire a female vice president. Fast."

But he didn't want a VP. If he couldn't trust his own family, how could he trust someone else with his company?

Hailey glanced over her shoulder to look in Michael's office again. Michael, Mason, and Trent had been in there since before she'd arrived to work an hour ago. What was up?

Whatever it was, Michael didn't look happy. In the short time she'd known him, she'd never seen him look so distressed. What could possibly be so terrible? From everything she'd seen as she learned the ins and outs of the company the business was solid. Then again, she'd yet to get her hands on an up-to-the-minute accounting of their finances. She'd only been given a prospectus that was outdated before it even hit her desk.

A raised voice filtered across the hall. Okay, she might be new, but she wasn't stupid. And if they kept this up everyone else would know their leaders were losing it. She stood, squared her shoulders and stepped across the hall. Not bothering to knock, she entered Michael's office. "Excuse me."

They didn't notice and kept up their arguing.

She raised her voice. "Excuse me."

They quieted and turned to her. Michael's eyes smoldered.

Maybe coming in here had been a bad idea after all. "I'm sorry to barge in, but your office isn't soundproof, and if you get any louder, everyone else is going to hear too."

Michael sighed. "Thank you, Hailey. I think we're done."

Mason stormed past her. She looked to the twins for an explanation.

"You better close the door and come have a seat."

Her heart skipped a beat. She did as he asked.

"You signed the confidentiality agreement?" Michael asked.

"Yes. My first day." She wished he'd get to the point. The coffee she'd had with breakfast was eating away at the lining of her stomach. If he didn't spit out the problem soon, she was liable to get an ulcer.

"Mason is taking an indefinite leave of absence."

"O-kay? Is he sick?"

He looked healthy to her, but she couldn't imagine any other reason for him to leave with no firm return date.

Trent sat on the corner of Michael's desk. "What

you're about to hear must never be repeated."

"I understand, but you're making me very nervous. What's going on?"

"Mason has a gambling problem. He's been to counseling, and we believed he had stopped, but Trent discovered otherwise. Long story short, we have a serious situation. He's been pilfering company funds to pay his gambling debts. So much so that making payroll next month is questionable unless something drastic happens."

She sagged against the back of the seat. "I gave up a great job to come here."

Trent leaned forward and rested a hand on her shoulder. "Look at me. We have a plan, and you're the key."

"I'll do anything possible to help."

"We're counting on it." Trent looked to his brother. "Remember when I told you I had a meeting in Portland?"

"Yes."

"That contract, if we get it, is large enough to get this company back on track and solvent again."

"Awesome. But what if when Mason returns, he does the same thing again?"

"He won't. I contacted our attorney, and she's drawing up papers as we speak to remove Mason from the partnership."

"You're buying him out?"

"In a manner of speaking. The money he stole is substantial. I agreed not to press charges, and he agreed the amount taken is sufficient payment to buy him out."

"Wow. Are you going to get a new partner?"

"That's where you come in."

"Me?" She squeaked. She cleared her throat.

"Yes." Michael took a breath and let it out in a puff. "The owner of the company with the big contract suggested we have a woman as our VP. Although not stated, she implied she will sign the contract only if we have a female in that position."

Hailey looked at the brothers and pointed from one to the other. "That's crazy. So you want me to be the VP of MM Enterprises? I don't have a clue what a VP does. Why not hire someone who is qualified?"

"Because I don't want or need a VP. I need you to agree to take the title as VP but continue on as you are doing now but with some added responsibility. Since Mason is leaving, I'll divvy up his job responsibilities."

How would she manage that as well as her regular duties?

Michael cleared his throat. "I know this is asking a lot. But I'd like for you to be my VP. After thinking on the suggestion for a bit I think it's a good idea to have a female in leadership here. It will make our company more appealing to females."

"Wow. This is surreal." It was the opportunity of a lifetime, but was it an opportunity she should take? She could always find another job.

"Tell me about it." Michael ran a hand along the back of his neck. "It infuriates me that Mason put me in this position, and that I have to drag you into this mess, but you're my best option. You're familiar with the business, you're smart, and you have a ton of energy. Please say you'll do it."

She took a breath and let it out. "I'll consider your offer. But this is a lot to take in."

"Thank you." Trent stood and handed her a manila envelope. "Our offer is inside. I think you'll agree that it's generous, all things considered. Take the rest of the day to do what you need to do, but we will need an answer at the game tomorrow."

"Tomorrow? Why the rush?"

"We have a lot of people depending on us. We want to act fast so our client doesn't sign with some other company."

She stood. "Is there a back way out of here? I don't think I can walk past Ian without him knowing something is up."

Michael stood. "I'll take you."

"Let me grab my stuff." On shaky legs, Hailey crossed the hall to her office and quickly gathered her belongings then met Michael in the hall. They walked silently to the emergency exit and took the stairs down, neither speaking.

At the bottom Michael pushed the heavy metal door open and followed her into the lobby. "I'll give you a ride home so you don't have to take the bus."

"Thanks. I appreciate that, but I was going to my brother's gym. I need to talk to him and get his advice about your offer."

"I'm happy to take you there."

She nodded and allowed him to guide her through the lobby to the exit leading to the parking garage.

"Your brother owns The Ring Athletic Club, right?"

"Yes, how'd you know?"

"Ian's mentioned it a few times."

"Of course. Ray and Ian have been the best of friends for a long time. Do you mind if I fill him in on what's going on? I really need to talk to someone, and we can trust him."

"I suppose that would be okay." He pressed the unlock button on the key toggle. "This is me." He stopped beside a Lexus NX Hybrid.

"Nice car, but somehow I pictured you in a sports car or a practical sedan."

He frowned. "Why?" He opened her door.

"Beats me." She sank onto the plush seat and deeply breathed in the new car smell.

Michael eased behind the wheel, and a moment later they headed for the exit.

"It smells new."

"It is."

Would he lose his car if she refused to take the job? Surely there was another woman he could bring in as the VP. Someone better qualified. If she said no, would he be able to find someone fast enough and would she be out of a job altogether? "If I turn down this position will I still have a job?"

"I hadn't thought that far ahead. I'm really hoping you'll see what a great opportunity this is. Read the package."

She looked at the envelope in her lap. What could they possibly offer her that would make her want to devote so much time to MM Enterprises?

8

Hailey sat in her brother's upstairs office that had a window looking down onto the gym below. She'd sent Ray a text on the way over and had hoped he'd be free to talk. To her dismay, he was in the middle of something across town. She'd read through the package and now she waited. Michael had actually escorted her in and offered to wait, but she'd declined. He had a mess to clean up, and she wanted to have a private conversation with her brother.

Lord, what should I do? The offer is amazing, but the hours are intense. I like working forty-hour weeks. This promotion would seriously affect my quality of life.

The door to Ray's office swung open and her brother burst in. "I'm sorry you had to wait. I got here as fast as I could. What's wrong?"

"What makes you think something is wrong?"

"You should be at work, but instead, you're here."

"Good reasoning." She sat in one of the old chairs that looked like it came from the fifties and patted the one beside her. "Join me. This is a conversation best had while sitting."

He frowned but sat.

She told him everything then waited. The clock on the wall ticked loudly in the silence. She couldn't take the quiet a moment longer. "I told Michael I needed to think about it."

"What's there to think about? It's an amazing opportunity. What's bothering you?"

"I'm still learning my job and the ins and outs of the company. How am I supposed to take over tasks one of the owners did? I'm going to fail, and I hate failing."

"Then don't fail. You can do this, Hailey."

She looked at her brother's sincerity-filled eyes. "How do you know?"

"Because when you put your mind to something, no matter how difficult or seemingly impossible, you always manage to succeed. Look at how you pulled off my wedding on such short notice."

"There's a big difference between a wedding and taking on this job."

He chuckled. "Tell me about it. But you have this. It's in your blood."

Maybe he was right. Her family had been running The Ring for generations. She'd grown up around businessmen and women and could hold her own with the best of them. "I think what's bothering me the most is that I feel obligated to do this. They are basically stuck thanks to Mason's actions, and now Michael has to do this to land a much needed contract."

"If you really don't want to take the job then don't, but what will happen to MM Enterprises?"

"I don't know. I guess they'd fold." She didn't want that to happen because she refused to take a promotion.

"How much money are we talking to keep them solvent?"

She shrugged. "Right now they can't meet payroll next month."

Ray blew out a breath. "I could probably give them a loan if you decide you don't want to do this."

"Why would you do that? You don't owe them anything."

"True, but I know what it's like to be in a tricky spot, and I'd like to help Michael if you decide to pass on the job."

"Now I'll feel extra guilty if I don't take the job." Talk about feeling pressured. If she took the job everyone would be happy, except maybe her. If she didn't, then her brother was out a ton of money and life would go on as usual. She didn't want Ray involved. But she'd unwittingly involved him by coming here. She sighed.

"Are you at all concerned that people in the office will assume you slept your way to the top?"

"That never crossed my mind, and I'm shocked you would think it. You sound like Mom."

"Gee thanks. That was a low blow."

She shrugged. "Sorry." But he did sound like her. Their mom would have said the exact same thing only with added drama and flare. "What do I do, Ray?"

"I think you should seriously consider the promotion. If you ultimately decide against it, come work for me. You just started there. You shouldn't feel obligated to them."

He was right, but that didn't change how she felt. "There's something else you should know. Before I found out Michael was my boss, we had really hit it off. In fact, if he hadn't asked me out before we arrived in Seattle, I'd planned to ask him."

"What are you saying?"

"I don't know. It probably doesn't matter that I was and still am attracted to him. I think the feeling is mutual but he won't go there." Would anything change if she was his vice president, or would he be even more determined to keep things professional?

"The two of you need to have a serious talk, and I think you need to pray. This is a big opportunity, and I'd hate to see you make a knee-jerk response and regret it later. Nonetheless, I'm willing to help Michael make payroll if that will buy him some time."

She sucked in a sharp breath. Her brother made a valid point. She needed to pray and consider the consequences of taking the job or not. But first a heart-to-heart with Michael was in order. She stood. "Thanks for being a sounding board."

"Where are you going?"

"I'm going to text Michael and see if he can meet with me sometime today. Then I'm going to go shoe shopping." There had to be another way to save the business.

"Why shoe shopping?"

"Retail therapy. It helps me think. I'll send the bill to Michael." She was only teasing about the last part, but shoe shopping did help her think.

She shot off a text to Michael then checked the bus schedule. She had a fifteen-minute wait for the bus she needed. A text came in from Michael.

Stay put. I'll come get you.

Will do.

She raised her head. "He's coming to get me."

"Okay. If you need me, call."

"I will. Thanks." She turned toward the door then stopped and looked over her shoulder at Ray. "I'll see you at home later." She dropped her phone into her purse then headed downstairs to watch for Michael from the glass doors. What would she say to him when he got here? She stared through the glass door. A garbage truck roared along the road. A siren wailed in the distance. A kid on a skateboard zipped past.

Life moved along like any other day except for one problem. Today was not like any other day. Today was life changing.

Michael pulled up to the curb in a loading zone spot in front of The Ring Athletic Club. He looked in his mirror for a cop. The last thing he needed was a parking ticket. He shot off a text to let Hailey know he was waiting.

A second later she rushed outside then jumped into his car. "You made good time."

"Yes. Where do you want to go?"

"Shoe shopping."

"Where?" His head jerked in her direction.

"There's a great place not far from here. If you find a place to park, we can walk."

He signaled then pulled away from the curb.

"How'd things go with your attorney?"

"Fine. She's moving fast to protect us. I still can't believe Mason did this."

"Why not? You knew he had a gambling problem. Why give him access to company money?"

He sucked in a sharp breath. He wanted to snap at her, but she had every right to ask the question considering what he was asking her to do. "Mason is my cousin and one of my best friends. We grew up together. I thought I'd know if he was up to something. I thought wrong."

"Have you considered getting a loan to tide the company over?"

"Trent is looking into that possibility. He's also checking with one of our investors who he believes might be sympathetic to our situation."

"My brother offered to help cover payroll, but I don't think he'd be able to cover all of it. He does well, but I don't think he realizes what software engineers make."

Surprise shot through him. "You told your brother about Mason?"

"I had to. I told you I needed his advice, and he needed the whole story."

His grip tightened on the steering wheel as he braked for a red light. So much for her confidentiality agreement, but she *had* asked permission first. It was his fault for granting it. "What did you tell him?"

"Everything I know. He's my brother and a business owner. He's done well for himself. You can trust him. I do."

He nodded, understanding why she'd tell him but still annoyed she'd told her brother so much. The entire mess was embarrassing. "Did he give you any advice?" The light changed and he accelerated.

"He said I needed to pray. He also said he believed in me, and that I could do anything I put my mind to."

He knew he'd liked Ray when he'd met him at the train station. The man clearly cared about his sister. He pulled into a vacant spot and set the brake. He waited for traffic to clear then darted around his vehicle and opened the passenger door for Hailey.

She stepped out. "Thanks. It's not far from here." She led the way. "My concern is that I just started at MM Enterprises. I'm still learning the company."

"What better way to learn than by taking over for Mason. You'll be working with our clients on a daily basis. Making sure we understand their needs as well as setting up any needed travel for Trent."

"But I don't know the first thing about engineering software. How can I possibly do what Mason does?"

"All you need to be able to do is communicate the

client's needs to our staff. They will take it from there."

"You should know my brother also offered me a job if I felt like I could no longer work for you."

Michael's insides jolted. He hadn't considered she'd choose to leave the company. Her brother seemed to have her back no matter what her decision. Even though he didn't want a VP to begin with, there was no one else besides Hailey he wanted to fill the role. "Wouldn't you be working below your potential there?"

"Yes, but it would only be temporary until I could find something in my field." She stopped outside a small store. "This is it. I haven't been here in years. I'm glad it's still around." She pushed on the glass door and entered the shop. She headed for a wall of shoes, and in a matter of minutes had several pairs in her hands.

A sales woman approached them. "Good morning, or rather afternoon. Would you like to try those on?"

"Yes, please. I wear a thirty-nine."

The woman took the collection of shoes that Hailey had gathered and headed into the stock room.

"I didn't know women's shoes came so big."

She chuckled. "These are European shoes. They're sized differently."

"I see." Didn't make sense why shoe size wasn't universal, but it was inconsequential. "Do you have any more questions for me?"

"I'm sure I'll think of some."

The woman came back with four boxes stacked in her arms. "Here we go."

Fifteen minutes later Hailey wore her new pair of

shoes. The sales woman said they were Mary Jane's with a low pump. "Now I'm ready to walk and talk. I want to help you, but I don't want to make a fool of myself in the process. I need to feel confident that I can do what you're asking of me."

"You won't look like a fool. If I didn't think you could do the job, I wouldn't have offered it to you."

"Really? I guess I assumed you only offered it to me because I was convenient."

"Not even close. I don't think you realize your full potential."

"And you do?" She raised a brow.

"Probably not, but I've seen what you've accomplished in your first week, and I'm impressed. You're smart and you're a people person. That combination will take you far in business." Had he laid it on too thick? He meant every word, but he didn't want her to think he was only flattering her.

"Thanks. I really appreciate you telling me that."

He grinned. "Would you like to grab lunch?"

"I don't think I could eat. Besides, playing hooky with the boss will get tongues wagging if word gets back to the office."

He didn't want to cause either of them embarrassment. "Trent decided to work from home today. Come to our house, and we'll get you up to speed on everything Mason did. Then you can make a fully-informed decision."

"I don't know if that's a good idea."

"You don't trust us?" It hurt that after all he'd said

and offered her she still didn't trust him.

"I wouldn't work for you if I didn't, but...never mind. Let's go. At least there we won't run the risk of bumping into someone on their lunch break."

"Exactly." He had guided them back to his car and stopped beside it. He opened her door then waited for traffic to clear and got behind the wheel.

He shot a look in her direction. She clenched her hands in her lap and had her bottom lip sucked in. He sighed mentally. He hated pulling her into the middle of this mess, but he had no other idea what to do about it. He didn't want to lose his company, and he didn't want to hurt Hailey. But could asking her to be his VP really be so bad?

9

Hailey stood on the front porch of the twins' house while they talked privately. Sunshine warmed her as she gazed at their mature yard with a large maple tree as the focal point. She hadn't expected they'd live together, but with all the traveling Trent did, it seemed reasonable he wouldn't need his own place. The men talked in low tones inside, and she could only capture snippets of their conversation. She gathered enough to know that Michael was filling Trent in on why she was at their home.

It sounded as though Trent was trying to find a new investor, so they could avoid taking on Mrs. Morris as a client. Would that take care of the problem, or had Mason's theft done too much damage? She really needed to see the current books. What she'd been looking at had been at least a month old. It was her job to guide these men, her job to make recommendations on where to expand, how to grow their business, where their resources should go. She should have thought of this sooner, but she'd been in shock. Now it was time to use the brain God gave her.

She turned, rapped on the door, and went inside without being invited. The brothers stood near the doorway. "Excuse me. I think we are going about this all wrong."

Michael frowned. "What do you mean?"

She motioned toward a sitting area. "May I?"

The twins nodded in unison and led the way. They sat on the sofa, leaving a black leather club chair open for her.

"You hired me to guide this business. Yet right now, I'm doing the following and being left out of the loop. I can't do my job if I don't have all the facts. Which means I need current numbers and information on all your projects and investors. What if I can turn this around without taking Mrs. Morris as a client?"

Trent grinned. "That'd be awesome. But are you sure? It's not pretty."

"I didn't expect it would be after what I've learned today, but this is why Michael and Mason hired me. Let me do my job. If in the end, I think the best way to move forward is to become entangled with Mrs. Morris, then I'll accept the promotion. But for now, I need information. All of it."

Wide-eyed, Michael looked to his brother. "She makes a good point."

"Yep. What do you want to do?"

"Let her do her job. How much time do we have before Mrs. Morris moves on?"

"One week," Trent said.

Hailey winced. That wasn't much time to restructure if needed. Good thing she had an ace up her sleeve. Ray had been running their grandfather's gym for years. And in the process, he'd taken a historic and aging boxing ring into the twenty-first century by purchasing the entire building and making the main level a state of the art athletic club. If anyone knew how to be creative, it was her brother. Michael scrubbed his hand over his face. "If we're going to do this we need to head back to the office."

Hailey stood. "Works for me."

"You sure?" Michael asked. "I said you could take the rest of the day off."

"As if. I haven't stopped working since I left the building." She grinned. "Come on gentlemen, we have a company to save."

Michael sat in his office, trying to focus on his computer screen, but his attention kept drifting across the hall to Hailey. She was something. He'd given her everything she'd asked for, and she'd been at it for hours. Five o'clock had come and gone an hour ago, and they were the only ones left in the office. Trent said he'd done all he could and needed a break so he left with the rest of the staff.

Michael stood then walked across the hall and

poked his head into Hailey's office. "How's it going?"

"I'm making progress, but not as much as I'd like."

"It's past six. I know for a fact you skipped lunch. How about we grab a bite and call it a night?"

"I'm fine. I've had some almonds. You go." She kept her focus on the computer screen.

He couldn't leave her here. For starters, she didn't have a key. Only he and Mason did. Correction only he and Trent did now. "Tell you what. I'll get us dinner, so you can keep working. What would you like?"

"Anything is fine."

"Okay. I'll grab a couple of subs and be right back."

"Thanks."

He'd lock up on the way out, so no one could disturb her. He frequented the sub sandwich shop at least once a week for lunch. Not exactly what he wanted for dinner on a Friday night, but it would have to do. He ordered a turkey club and a black forest ham.

Michael headed back to the office, took the elevator up, then went into the office, locking up behind him. There was no reason anyone should be coming in at this hour. It was nearing seven o'clock. He went into her office without knocking. "Would you like turkey club or black forest ham?"

"They both sound delicious. Whichever one you don't want, I'll eat."

He sat across from her desk and studied her. Her brow wrinkled as her lips moved silently. In a word, she was adorable. "Hey. Stop working for a bit and eat." He slid her the turkey sub.

"No time. I only have a week to save this company."

He frowned. "Hailey." He waited for her to look up. "It will keep for five minutes. Please eat."

Surprise flickered in her eyes. "Okay. What do I owe you?"

"My treat." He unwrapped his meal and waited for her to do the same. He wouldn't let her get away with not eating. He shot up a silent blessing for his food then dug in, grinning when Hailey did the same. Progress.

"Mason is a smart man. If your brother hadn't been looking in the right spot, Mason might have drained MM Enterprises dry. As it is, I think there's hope."

Relief washed over him. "That's the best news I've heard all day." He took a bite of his sandwich.

"If we can get a loan to cover payroll next month, and drum up a couple of new contracts we'll be able to make up for the loss."

And there went his appetite. "Trent looked into getting a loan from several lenders today. It's not an option."

"Seriously?"

He nodded. "I'm sure you'll figure out why as you dig into our financials. As far as getting more business goes, it would take several accounts to make up that kind of loss."

"Or the contract with Mrs. Morris?" She raised her brow as she took a small bite from her sandwich.

"Yes."

She sighed. "I'm beginning to understand."

"Are you giving up?"

"No way. As flattered as I am that you'd offer to make me your VP, I'm not crazy about being married to my job. And like I mentioned before, my brother seemed open to loaning you money."

He shook his head. "If a bank or credit union won't extend credit to us, I wouldn't feel right accepting it from your brother. Clearly we're a high risk."

"Are you good for it?"

"Right now...I don't know." For the first time in his life he didn't know what to do. *Lord, please show me the way.*

Hailey swallowed the dry sandwich and wished for a glass of water. She stood. "Be back in a minute." She filled a cup from the water cooler near the reception desk, guzzled it and refilled it and another one for Michael.

Fatigue struck her, and she suddenly realized the time. Her brother must be worried sick. She rushed back to her office. "I brought you some water. I didn't realize it was so late." She reached for her phone. "The battery is dead." She pulled a charger from her top desk drawer and plugged it in. "Just as I thought. Ray has been trying to reach me." She shot off a quick text, letting him know she was fine and working late."

Do you need a ride home?

"Everything okay?" Michael asked.

"Yes. My brother wants to know if I need a ride. The busses are still running, right?"

"Yes, but tell him I'll give you a ride."

"You sure?"

"Yes. The sooner you get home the better. Our softball game is in the morning, and you need a good night's sleep."

"About that. I didn't get as much practice in as I'd hoped."

"Your ability to catch a ball is the least of my worries, Hailey. Maybe by Monday we'll have found a way out of this mess."

Right, the time crunch. It hadn't occurred to her to work over the weekend. "I need a key."

"If you're in the office, I'll be here too. I'll give you a ride over after the game tomorrow morning."

"Okay." At least she didn't have anything else on her agenda, except brunch with her mom on Sunday. "I can't work Sunday."

"That's fine."

She wrapped her half-eaten sandwich and stood. "You ready to head out?"

"More than."

What a week! If her first week had been so nuts what would her second hold?

10

Hailey sat between Savannah and Paige in the dugout. Their team was last at bat. They were down by two. According to the rules of their league everyone was in the batting order even if they didn't field. They had one out, and she was on deck after the next batter.

Hailey jiggled the bench slightly with her bouncing leg. "You nervous?" Paige asked.

"I don't want to let the team down." Hailey kept her gaze on the batter.

"Remember to keep your eyes open and watch the ball," Paige said.

"Keep my eyes open. Got it." That hadn't helped her last two times at bat, but she'd try extra hard this time.

The metal bat struck the ball, and Ian raced to first base. The crowd in the stands clapped and shouted encouragement. She heard Brandi above the rest and chuckled. Ian's wife had lungs.

Paige tugged on her arm. "You're on deck. Make sure you wear a batting helmet and stay in the circle while you take a few practice swings. Keep your eye on the ball."

"Even if I'm only practicing?"

"Yes. It's the rule. That's why the umpire yelled at you last time. And get out of the way of a foul ball this time."

"Right. Eye on the ball." She stood and put on the helmet then grabbed a bat and did as instructed. The bat made contact with the ball again, and someone whose name she didn't recall charged to first.

"You're up, Hailey," Paige shouted. "Eye on the ball."

The bases were loaded, and she was up to bat. Talk about pressure. How had this happened? At least they only had one out. When the ball came at her, she jumped away.

"Stay in the box," the umpire warned.

"Sorry." She copied what the batters before her had done and managed to stay in the box this time as the ball came at her. She closed her eyes and swung.

"Strike!"

"Come on, Hailey you can do this." Michael stood at third. "Bring us home."

She took a deep breath and let it out then stood at ready. The ball arched toward her. She stared at it then swung. *Smack!* Her hands stung.

"Run!" someone shouted.

She dropped the bat and charged to first.

"Keep going." The base coach waved her on.

She ran to second and heard everyone shouting at her to run, so she ran to third and kept going.

"Slide!" Someone shouted.

How? Her heart pounded as she bent her legs and dropped, sliding to home plate. *Ouch.* At least nothing felt broken. She coughed as fine dirt swirled around her. She'd need a shower after this. She lay on her side as craziness ensued. Suddenly she was being pulled to her feet and hoisted onto Trent's and Michael's shoulders. "Whoa. Put me down."

The men carefully lowered her to the ground. "You did it! We won." Michael's smile lit his face. "I could kiss you."

Her heart skipped. Had anyone heard? She sure hoped not. She looked around, and no one seemed to have noticed his comment. Whew. Even if they had, they probably thought nothing of it. Unlike her, who hoped he really meant it.

Trent and Michael positioned themselves by her sides. Her body hurt in places she didn't know could hurt, yet she didn't care. It was worth it to see how happy everyone was, especially with all that was going on with the company.

She turned to Michael. "I need to go home and shower, then I'll meet you at the office."

"The team usually goes out together after the game. You're the MVP. You should be there."

"Me? I only hit the ball once."

"And won us the game." He grinned.

She stood a little taller. "I don't know. I should probably get to the office as soon as possible."

"I'd like you to be there, but I can't force you to go out with us. Sure you won't change your mind? Work will keep for an hour."

It did sound like fun. She craned her neck, looking for Paige. She called out to her sister-in-law. "Have you seen Paige?"

Katie raised her hands in a shrug.

"Everything okay?" Michael asked.

"I don't know. Now that the dust has cleared, I don't see my friend. If I'm going to this thing, I want her to come too. Excuse me." She strode to the dugout and spotted Paige bent over gathering her stuff. "There you are. Everyone gets together after the game. You want to go?"

"Sure. How are you feeling? That was a nasty-looking slide."

Hailey rubbed the outside of her thigh. "I'll live. You need to teach me how to slide."

"First thing Monday night."

"Uh...no. Let's give it a week."

Paige laughed. "Probably a good idea." She hoisted her bag onto her shoulder. "Where're we going?"

"Let's go find out."

They joined the team and their families by the bleachers right as the group began to disperse. She caught up to Katie. "Where's everyone going?"

"They decided to pass on a party."

"Why?" Disappointment shot through her even

though five minutes ago she didn't want to go.

"It's a sunny Saturday in Seattle, and those with kids had already made plans."

"Oh. I guess that makes sense. What are you and Ray up to today?"

"The zoo. You're welcome to join us."

"I wish I could, but I have something I need to do today. Have fun." She turned to where she'd left Paige and spotted her talking with one of the twins. Since they were in uniform, it was hard to tell who was who without hearing their voices. She walked over to them.

"Thanks for joining the team today. You're a great fielder," Trent said.

Paige grinned. "I had fun."

"Will you be joining us next week?"

Hailey held in a giggle. Her friend had a sparkle in her eyes reserved for special people. Hmm. She held back, not wanting to interrupt. She didn't know Trent well enough to know if he was interested in her friend for anything more than a ballplayer.

A moment later Paige noticed her standing there. "You ready?"

"Mm-hmm. See you, Trent." They walked toward Paige's car. "Thanks for today. I wouldn't have survived without you."

"I highly doubt that. But I'm glad I came. Trent is cute. I see why you're attracted to his brother."

"Shh." She looked around to make sure no one was close enough to overhear. Thankfully, few people were still there. Michael and Trent headed for their vehicles on the other side of the park.

"What's going on with you?" Paige asked. "You haven't been yourself today."

"Haven't I? It's probably nerves about the game."

"I don't think so. This is something different."

"When did you become a psychologist?"

"Cute. It doesn't take being a psychologist for a girl to know when something's up with her best friend."

"I'm fine. But I love you for caring so much." Hailey did not want to have this conversation with Paige—she wasn't ready. It was crazy how she could talk to her brother or Michael about it, but not Paige. Maybe it was because Paige knew her too well.

"When you're ready to talk, let me know."

"I will." This was exactly why Paige was her BFF. Now to clean up and face the source of her problems.

Michael waited near the door to the office for Hailey. She'd sent him a text a short time ago saying she was on her way up. And there she was. She'd washed her hair, and it hung in damp ringlets past her shoulders. Her dressed-down look of leggings and a long T-shirt was quite a change from her usual professional suits but looked good on her. He pulled the door open for her then locked it. "Thanks for coming in on a Saturday."

"You ready for this?"

No. "Ready as I'll ever be. Let's hammer this out."

He brought his laptop and worked from a corner in her office, so he'd be nearby if she had questions. From time to time he looked up and caught her grinning. Did she enjoy trying to find money where there was none?

Two hours later she pushed back from her desk. "I need a break." She rolled her neck and stood. "Let's get out of here for a bit."

"Really?" He figured she'd work until he forced her to go home.

"Yes. My brain is sluggish. I need a change in scenery."

"Sounds good to me." Who was he to question the woman that might possibly save his business? If she said she needed a break, then a break she would have. "Want to walk down to the water?"

"I guess."

"Not your thing?" He pulled open the door then locked up behind them while she pressed the elevator button.

"I love the water. It's walking back up the hill that I'm not crazy about. Don't tell anyone I said this, but my body hurts in places I didn't know could hurt."

"The game. I should've thought of that. Did you injure yourself, or are you just out of shape?" Maybe he shouldn't have said that last part.

She playfully slugged his arm as the elevator doors slid open. "That wasn't nice."

He rubbed his arm. "Neither was punching me." He pressed the button for the ground floor.

"You think that hurt? Ha! You should see my leg."

"What's wrong with your leg?" Concern held him.

"It's nothing, only a shiner."

"I'm sorry. That was a rough slide."

"My first." The doors slid open, and they headed for the bank of glass doors leading to the sunshine. "I can't believe it's this gorgeous outside, and we're holed up in a windowless office."

"I know, but we're outside now. So enjoy it while you can." He intended to relish every second. "I'm in the mood for seafood. How about you?"

"Sounds good to me. But let's find something easy so we can eat and walk."

"Clam chowder?"

"On a summer day?" She shrugged. "Sure. Why not?" Cars zipped past as they joined a sea of bodies along the sidewalk. "I wish I had good news to give you. But so far a contract with Mrs. Morris is the best thing that could happen to your company."

His mood plummeted—he really didn't want to have anything to do with that manipulative woman. Even the sunshine and good company didn't help. "You looked so hopeful when you were working today. I thought things were looking up."

"There were times I was hopeful, then I dug deeper. When we get back, I'll keep at it, but short of a flurry of new contracts or someone giving you a large loan, I think you need Mrs. Morris."

He almost growled but caught himself. He stopped walking, and the person behind him bumped into him and made a rude comment before walking on. He pulled

Hailey off to the side out of the flow of foot traffic. "Are you willing to take on the VP job? That's the only way this will work."

"I'm not ready to commit. I'm doing my job and advising you what's best for your company. Honestly, Michael, working the kind of hours I'd need to work doesn't sound like much of a life."

He nodded. She was right. They'd both be working more hours since they'd be doing the job of one and a half people. Plus the learning curve would slow them down. If he thought bringing in an experienced outsider would be a better option than Hailey, he'd do it in a heartbeat, but he had no doubt Hailey was the woman for the job—now to convince her of that.

"We could make it fun."

She chuckled. "How would we do that?"

"I'll work on it and get back to you. What do we do now though?"

"Now?" She looped her hand through his arm. "You feed me." She pulled him back into the flow of foot traffic.

He looked down at their linked arms. Clearly she felt comfortable with him, which he was grateful for, but her boldness surprised him to silence.

She stopped at a food window and released his arm. "Two bowls of clam chowder please."

In a daze he pulled out his wallet and paid. "I'm beginning to think you're a godsend."

She chuckled. "Why's that?"

They walked slowly in the direction they'd come.

"You give me hope. If you hadn't been here when Trent discovered what Mason had done, I think I might have handed out pink slips already." He needed this woman, and he never needed anyone. Well maybe he did need people, but he needed her in a different way. She inspired him to be better, smarter, and stronger.

"Then I'm glad I'm here, at least for now."

"What does that mean?" He frowned.

"If this deal with Mrs. Morris goes awry and you can't secure a loan, then I'm out of a job."

No matter what, he couldn't let that happen.

11

Hailey stared in a daze at the wall in her apartment after a long day. Her leg throbbed from sliding into home plate, and her eyes burned from too much computer time. Between the game and then working with Michael, today had been one big roller coaster. The more time she spent with him the more she wanted to be with him.

A knock at her door drew her attention. She stood and unlocked it. "Hi, Ray. Come in."

"Good job at the game today."

"Thanks. I got lucky."

"Yep."

She slugged his shoulder playfully. "If you came here to insult me, you can leave."

"Sorry. No, I wanted to see if you decided to take the promotion."

She should have known this conversation was coming. "Have a seat. I'll make us some tea."

"None for me. I'm more of a hot chocolate

person."

"Since when?"

He shrugged. "Katie has rubbed off on me."

"I guess so. As it happens, your wife supplied me with cocoa mix. I presume for these late-night visits. Want some?"

"I'll pass this time."

"Suit yourself." She joined him on the couch. "I'm leaning toward accepting the position, but we still have to get a signed contract from Mrs. Morris."

"What made you change your mind? Last we spoke you were solidly against it."

"Something Michael said. Plus, I realized I'm not in this alone. Michael is putting in as much effort as me, and I can always go to him if I'm having a problem. Then there's the package they offered if I take the job, and if the deal goes through it's great. I could afford a condo on the water if I wanted."

"Is that what you want?"

"I don't know, but options are nice." When she'd first come home she thought she knew what she wanted. Funny how quickly things changed. "We're going to call Mrs. Morris on Monday to set up a meeting with her at her office in Portland. Trent, Michael, and I will all drive down together so she can meet me."

"Why are all of you going? Seems like overkill. Aren't you afraid the woman will get a bigger head than she already has?" He looked curious more than concerned.

"Trent has established a relationship with her, so he

will be there. I have no idea why Michael is going. I didn't question his reason."

"Interesting. With all that's going on, I doubt he can afford a day away from the office right now. I think he cares for you. He wouldn't have suggested tagging along otherwise."

She shook her head. "We have chemistry, but—"

"Don't deny it. I saw the two of you at the game today. There's something there whether either of you wants to admit it or not."

She blew out a quick breath. "You are so annoying sometimes."

He laughed. "Back at you. Don't forget we're having brunch with Mom tomorrow after church."

"Right." She'd forgotten. "Can I ride with you?"

"Of course. See you in the morning."

She walked him to the door and locked up, doubting she'd sleep, regardless of how tired she was. Her brain ran at lighting speed and wouldn't slow. Now she had her mom to worry about. Too bad she couldn't put her off for a week. But there was no point in prolonging the inevitable.

Hailey sat across from her brother at the formal dining room table in their mother's house. It reminded her of episodes of the Gilmore Girls when Lorelai and Rory were having their weekly dinner at Lorelai's parents'

home. Except Hailey wasn't witty and capable of a rapid-fire conversation that could make a person's head spin.

"Your brother tells me you have a prestigious job at a software development company."

Hailey reached for her water goblet. "That's correct. In fact, I'm up for a promotion."

"So fast. That's impressive. I always knew you were a smart girl. At least that expensive college education I paid for is good for something."

"Thanks." It seemed her mother couldn't resist a jab, even when attempting a compliment. Which was sad. She looked to Ray, hoping he'd fill in the silence. She wanted to gain ground with their mom today, but she wasn't making it easy.

"What do you think of the caprese salad? The tomatoes are from my garden."

"They're delicious," Ray said.

"I agree. Some of the best I've had. How'd you get them to ripen so early?" Hailey skewered one with her fork.

"I started them in a hothouse."

"When did you take up gardening?" She didn't remember her mom ever working in the yard when she was growing up.

"My therapist suggested it last year."

"You see a therapist?"

"Yes. Do you have a problem with that?" Mom snapped.

"Not at all. I was just surprised. I'm sorry you felt judged."

Her mother dabbed the tip of her mouth with a napkin. "I'm sorry for snapping."

At least she was trying to be polite. That was a step up from when Ray had brought her here last time. "What else do you grow in your garden?"

"Peppers, corn, beans, yellow squash, zucchini, acorn squash, and a few blueberry bushes. They're covered in berries right now. I have to fight with the birds for my share."

Ray chuckled. "Katie has the same battle at our place. The kids love blueberries."

"You need to bring my grandchildren to see me more often. They'd enjoy my garden."

"I'll mention it to Katie."

Hailey listened to the exchange with wonder. Maybe showing up without calling last time had been the root of her mom's rudeness, because she seemed fine with Ray. "I've never tried gardening. After we eat will you show me yours?"

"We'll see. I'm meeting a friend."

Her mom had friends? She'd assumed she was a recluse. Her assumptions were wreaking havoc on her relationship with her mom. "Maybe another time then."

"I'd like that."

Hailey suppressed a grin. She didn't want Mom to think she was gloating, but she couldn't help feeling as if she'd won a round with her mother.

A short time later Hailey sat beside her brother as they headed home. "I thought today went okay. How about you?"

"It wasn't a disaster, that's for sure. With time, I think Mom might begin to lighten up."

"I hope you're right. I know she's never been a touchy-feely mother, but it would be nice if I didn't feel like I had to be so careful about everything I do and say when I'm with her. It's kind of stressful."

"Sure is. I've been there myself. I'm praying for your relationship with her."

"I appreciate that. You have any plans for the rest of your day?"

"Family time with the kids. Katie's mom is in town and—"

"Wait. I didn't know she had a relationship with her mom. I thought she was abandoned and that's why she grew up in foster care."

"Her mom showed up right before we got married. They've exchanged emails and met in person a few times. It's a strain on Katie to have her mom in town, but she wants to see her grandchildren so we're all going to the zoo."

"Wow. Guess I should be praying for Katie." It seemed when she left for Chicago she left a lot behind. "Why didn't I know any of this?"

"You were only nineteen when we married and had enough on your plate. I didn't want to burden you with anymore drama than you already had to deal with."

"I'm not nineteen anymore. It's okay to burden me."

He chuckled. "Seems to me you have your share of trouble to manage."

"I suppose, but I really don't want to think about work right now." Even though it was inevitable that she'd have to deal with it, she wanted today off.

"I understand. Do you want to come to the zoo with us?"

"I'll pass, but thanks for asking. What I need is to soak in a hot tub. I'm so sore from the game yesterday."

"As it happens, we have one."

"What? Where?" How had she missed it?

"It's off the side of the house. You can't see it because there's a privacy fence around it, but you can access it from my study. You're welcome to use it anytime Katie and I aren't."

"Cool. Thanks."

They pulled into the driveway then went their separate ways. Ray was a great brother, and not for the first time, she was grateful for him. She dug out her swimsuit, slipped on flip-flops, grabbed a towel and made a beeline for that hot tub. At the bottom of her stairs she froze. Michael's car was in the driveway, and he was getting out of it. Why, oh why, had she not worn a cover up? "Michael, this is a surprise." She wrapped the towel around her waist.

"Your brother asked me to stop by."

So he wasn't here for her—too bad. "Oh. He didn't mention it to me."

He shrugged. "Are you going swimming?"

"Hot tub. You might as well follow me. I'll get Ray for you." Her sandals flopped against her heels as she led the way to the kitchen door everyone used as a front entrance since it was adjacent to the driveway. She rapped on the door, then let herself in. "Ray," she called out.

"In the living room."

"Michael is here to see you."

They'd probably meet in Ray's study, which meant they'd have a direct view of her in the hot tub. Suddenly a soak didn't appeal.

Ray stopped short in the doorway to the kitchen. "I guess I should have mentioned I asked Michael over."

"Yes. You should have." She smiled sweetly. "I'll come back later." She fled from the house.

Michael hoped his face wasn't as red as it felt. Talk about awkward. Ray should've warned Hailey. The kitchen door smacked closed.

Ray blew out a breath. "I'm sorry about that. She mentioned wanting to use the hot tub, but I didn't realize she would come over before we left."

"You're leaving?"

"In about an hour. This won't take long. Let's talk in my office." Ray led the way to a room along the side of the house.

The office was simple with a single desk, a couch, and a wall of storage. If he had to guess, he'd say the couch held a hide-a-bed and the room doubled as a guest room.

"Thanks for coming on such short notice." Ray

motioned to a chair. "Have a seat."

"Thanks. What's this about?" He figured it had something to do with his business since Hailey had consulted with him.

"My sister said you were unable to get a traditional loan and you're unwilling to take one from me."

"True." Unease snaked its way through him.

"I'd like you to reconsider my offer if the contract doesn't go through."

"I don't understand why you'd want to help me. I'm a huge risk. I might not be able to pay back the loan."

"I'd do about anything to help my sister and my best friend. They both like working for you. I've done my research. Were it not for your shyster business partner, you'd be doing quite well. Based on what I've seen and heard about you, I have faith that you're good for the money. If things don't go as you hope this week, know that you can count on me to cover your payroll."

He opened his mouth, and no sound came out. How could this man put so much faith in him when he didn't have it in himself? He cleared his throat. "I appreciate your incredibly generous offer."

"But?"

"But let's wait and see what happens this week. Your sister worked out a solid presentation. I'm praying things will go in our favor and we sign a big client." He didn't like the other options—closing his company or borrowing money from Hailey's brother. The more he thought about it the more he liked the idea of giving Hailey added responsibility.

12

Hailey grabbed her backpack purse then headed out. Paige was tagging along today to see some sites in Portland while they were in their meeting since Michael couldn't come with them after all. Hailey waved to her friend who was sitting behind the wheel of her Honda.

Paige got out and stood between the door and her car. "Hurry up, girl. I don't want Trent to think I made you late."

"Shh. You'll wake up the neighborhood." She tossed her purse onto the backseat then secured her seatbelt.

"Oops." Paige ducked back into the car.

"Did you plug Trent's address into your GPS?"

"Yes, and thanks for inviting me to come along. I'm looking forward to checking out Portland. There's so much to see there."

"You won't have a lot of time for sightseeing. I don't expect our meeting to go longer than an hour."

"Phooey. That's not enough time." Paige backed out

of the driveway and headed for Trent's place.

"I know. Maybe Trent will be willing to do a little sightseeing after the meeting."

"I hope so. What happened with Michael? Why'd he bail?"

"There was really no reason for him to be there. Since I accepted the position as his VP with the understanding this deal had to go through to make it permanent, his time is better spent at the office. Especially since Mason is no longer part of the business."

"I see. It's too bad though. It would've been fun to have Michael along."

Because of her confidentiality agreement she couldn't tell Paige the full story. "Yeah. But he really needs to be at the office in case something comes up." She wished he were coming too. They'd been working so closely over the past few days he'd quickly become a fixture in her life. She'd miss him.

"Is this it?" Paige ducked and peered through the windshield.

"Yep."

"Okay." She parked.

Hailey grabbed her backpack and got out.

Paige trotted around the car wearing her own fashion backpack and grinning. "This is going to be so much fun."

Trent walked outside and met them beside Paige's car. "Good morning. Are you ladies ready?"

"Yes!" Paige practically burst with enthusiasm.

Trent shot Hailey a look that made her snort laugh. "She's not normally like this. In fact, Paige isn't even a morning person."

"Could've fooled me." He chuckled and led them to his no-frills SUV.

"I get motion sick. Do you mind if I sit in front?" Paige asked.

"Go for it," Trent said.

Paige bounded past them and hopped into the vehicle.

If her friend didn't get her excitement under control, Trent was liable to leave her here.

"What's up with Paige? She wasn't like that at the game." Trent spoke softly.

"I think she had way too much coffee. Remember? Not a morning person."

He nodded. "Got it. So she'll crash in what, an hour?"

"We can only hope." She slid into the pristine backseat. It looked unused, not so much as a gum wrapper or pine needle. He must not spend much time in his car. They'd gone over their plan for the meeting at least a dozen times since Monday so why was she nervous?

Trent got settled and headed for I-90 and flipped on the radio, which was tuned to K-Love—a pleasant surprise. Her body relaxed, and soon she was singing along with Paige to the radio. Trent caught her eye in the rearview mirror a few times. If the sparkle in his eyes meant what she thought, he was enjoying the entertainment. "The two of you should take your act on the road."

Paige laughed. "Only if you join us."

"Don't tempt me." He winked in the rearview mirror. Clearly he was having fun with Paige and wanted Hailey to know he was teasing.

Around Tacoma they settled down. Trent and Paige spoke quietly in the front, and with the road noise, she had no idea what they were talking about. She pulled out her phone and shot off a text to Michael.

Will let you know when I have a signed contract. How's it going at the office?

She watched the screen for his reply.

Typical day. Look forward to having the contract in hand. When you get back we'll celebrate. Dinner's on me. Tell Trent.

Will do. Talk to you later.

She laid the phone on the seat beside her, trying to ignore the disappointment. At first she'd thought he was taking her out, but of course he was all business as usual.

"You okay back there?" Trent's gaze met hers in the rearview mirror.

She forced a smile. "Great. Michael says dinner's on him when we get back, assuming the deal goes through as planned."

"Not that I'm complaining," Paige said, "but with all the technology we have, why is it you have to sign this in person?"

"I like to meet with our clients face to face. There's something to be said for being in the same room as a person," Trent said.

"I suppose." Paige didn't sound convinced.

They finally made it to Portland and dropped Paige downtown before heading to their meeting. They stood outside a tall building. Trent squared his shoulders. "You ready for this?"

"Absolutely. Lead the way."

He opened the door for her, and they headed for an elevator that whisked them to the fifth floor. It opened into a quiet hall.

"This way." Trent took a right out of the elevator then entered the first door they came to. He strode to the reception desk. "I'm Trent Pierce, and this is Hailey O'Brien here for our ten o'clock meeting with Mrs. Morris."

The brunette woman spoke on the phone. "Go down this hall. The conference room is the second door on the left."

"Thank you." He looked to Hailey. "Ready?"

She nodded, reminding herself to breathe. This was her first official act as vice president for MM Enterprises, and she didn't want anything to go wrong. Maybe a backpack purse was a poor choice, but this was Portland, Oregon where pretty much anything went.

A woman who appeared to be not much older than Hailey stood beside the table. She held out her hand to Trent. "It's good to see you again, Trent." She looked at Hailey. "And you must be the new VP I've heard so much about. Trent seems quite enamored with your skills."

Trent's eyes widened. "We appreciate you taking the

time to meet with us in person, Mrs. Morris, to finalize your contract." Trent moved to the single table in the center of the adequately sized room, placed a briefcase on it, then pulled out a document. "X marks the spots where we need you to sign. Would you like some time to look over the contract? Hailey and I could come back in an hour?"

"I went through the copy you emailed." Mrs. Morris smiled. "So long as nothing has changed I'm comfortable signing this after I visit with your new VP for a bit."

Hailey sucked in a quick breath. "Certainly. Shall we sit?" She found a spot at the table without waiting for her reply, trying to figure out this woman's game. Then again maybe she wasn't playing games and was sincere. She was tough to read. "I assume Trent explained that you'll be conferring with me about your software needs."

"He did. How much do you know about the software business?"

"Enough." She needed to pick Ian's brain, so if things got too technical she'd know what their clients were talking about. "Should you have concerns at any time, I'll be happy to talk with you about them."

They chatted for a little longer, then Mrs. Morris grabbed a pen and scribbled her signature in all the right places. She stood and offered her hand. "Thank you for taking the time out of your day to meet in person."

"It's been a pleasure." Hailey took the contract and handed it to Trent who had an incredibly pleased look on his face. She couldn't wait to see Michael's face when they gave it to him. She almost laughed at her silliness;

he'd look exactly like Trent did.

Michael sat across from his brother and Hailey at one of his favorite steakhouses. He'd missed Hailey today. "Tell me what you think of Mrs. Morris, Hailey."

"She's fine. I thought she'd be eccentric, considering she demanded you have a woman in leadership at your company, but she's an average woman. Did she wire the money?"

Michael looked to his brother, who handled the books.

"It's in our account. We'll be able to make payroll without a problem and keep the lights on."

"That was a problem too?" A stricken look engulfed Hailey's face.

Michael chuckled. "He was trying to be funny. I'm sure we had enough to cover the utilities." He shot his brother a look that warned him to not disagree. Though intelligent, Hailey was a little gullible at times. It had been a long day for all of them, so he wanted to give her a break.

She ducked her chin. "Paige had fun today. Thanks for letting her come along."

"Sure. She's great. I can see why you're friends." Trent faced his brother. "You should have heard the two of them singing at the top of their lungs with the radio."

Michael raised his brows. "Too bad I missed that."

He couldn't imagine, then again maybe he could. Hailey was definitely multi-dimensional. Their food came, and he offered up a quick blessing.

Hailey cut into her steak. "This looks delicious. Thanks."

He nodded and took a bite of his perfectly-cooked prime rib. *Mmm.* Now that was melt-in-your-mouth perfection. Tonight had been a good idea for so many reasons. Not the least of which was the opportunity to spend a relaxing evening, not working, with Hailey. They'd have to do this again sometime. Alone.

"I'm looking forward to the game this weekend." Trent forked a bite of mashed potatoes into his mouth and quickly swallowed. "I'm adding Paige to the roster."

This was the first Michael had heard. "Did Savannah quit the team?"

"She turned in her jersey yesterday." Trent loaded his fork with a slice of juicy steak.

"I'm sorry Savannah quit," Hailey said. "I'd hoped she'd stick it out."

Trent shook his head. "I think as soon as she saw that Paige knew what she was doing she quit mentally."

"Yeah." Michael waved his fork. "I noticed that too. She really didn't want to be there last week. It's too bad. I think it's good for all of us to get out and have some fun together."

"Except it wasn't fun for Savannah," Hailey added. "If I were better at it, I might enjoy it, but I'll admit it wasn't much fun for me, either."

Michael rested his fork on the side of his plate.

"Then let me help coach you. Between Paige and me, we'll have you enjoying the game in no time."

"Count me in too," Trent said.

"I had no idea the two of you were such sports enthusiasts." Hailey reached for her water glass.

Trent was but Michael wasn't, not really—he was a computer nerd and generally left sports to his brother. But he liked to win so he'd always done his best when they were kids and learned to hold his own at whatever sport he tried—except soccer. He was terrible at that. Kicking a ball while running was not in his skill set.

Besides, any excuse to spend time with Hailey appealed. He shrugged off the thought—he was getting dangerously close to crossing his own line and asking her out. But now, more than ever, he needed to keep things in the friendship zone. She was his VP and neither of them could afford to complicate things by dating.

13

Hailey sat with Paige on the grass in the park near the backstop one evening after work. Since the celebratory dinner two nights ago, they'd set up a practice session with Trent and Michael. Her fingers tingled in anticipation. Why was she so nervous?

Paige checked the time on her phone. "The guys are late."

"I noticed. Should we start without them?"

"Maybe. I don't know how long this field will be available. If it's reserved, a team could show up at any time and boot us off."

"Let them." Her heart wasn't into practicing tonight. It'd been a grueling day video conferencing with Mrs. Morris. She'd brought Ian in at one point since she literally had no idea what the woman was trying to tell her. Whatever made her think she could do that part of her job? Oh right, Michael convinced her, just like he'd gotten her to play softball. It was as if he had her under mind control. She chuckled at the ridiculous thought.

"What's so funny?" Paige squinted into the sunlight as she looked toward Hailey.

"Just letting my mind wander."

"And where did it go?" Her friend hugged her knees to her chest.

"My lips are sealed."

"You're no fun. But you know who is fun? Trent. You're so lucky to work with him."

Hailey shrugged. She worked more with Trent than Michael, which was good since she wasn't attracted to Trent, even though the men looked exactly alike.

"What's he like to work with? Is he as silly as he was when we were driving to Portland?"

"He's more serious at the office." Maybe if things weren't so tense there, she'd witness his playful side, but as it stood MM Enterprises was experiencing a huge shift. They'd lost one owner and gained a VP that had little idea what she was doing, aside from the job she'd been originally hired to do. She felt woefully inadequate. Hopefully that would change as she learned the business.

"I suppose being serious at work is a good thing, considering his job. I imagine a jokester wouldn't instill much faith in the company when he's talking to potential clients."

"Probably not."

"What's Michael like? Anything like his brother?"

"Only in looks. Michael is more serious. He gets excited about new technology, and he's super kind and considerate. He actually insisted I eat one night when we were working late. He's a gentleman in every sense of the word." Except that one time when he wouldn't let her walk to the office with him.

"Hmm. He sounds pretty wonderful. Maybe I have my eye on the wrong brother."

Hailey frowned.

Paige laughed. "Kidding. I'm not blind. I can see you have a thing for him."

"I do not have a *thing* for Michael."

"Did I hear my name?" Michael strolled over with Trent beside him.

Hailey's heart skipped a beat and she whirled around. "It's about time the two of you showed up. What happened?"

"Something came up at work."

"Oh? Anything I should be concerned about?"

"We'll talk tomorrow. In the meantime, let's get some practice in. I have the field reserved for another thirty minutes."

"*You* reserved the field?" Paige shook her head in disbelief. "I'm impressed."

"Don't be." Trent slid his hand into a glove. "It's the team's normal practice night, and we have it reserved for the season. We didn't consider that no one would want to practice once the games started."

"Oh." Clearly Paige wasn't as impressed as she had been.

Hailey stifled a chuckle, happy her friend had moved past her interest in Michael. She might not be able to have him, but she didn't want Paige to either. That would be too painful.

Thirty minutes later, the four of them packed up and headed for the parking lot. Paige strolled beside Trent. "You're pretty good at this, Trent. Did you play in high school or college?"

"Only high school. I hit the books back in college. What about you?"

"No sports in college, and I hit the books as well. I graduated recently with a degree in Marine Biology."

"Cool. What are you going to do with it?"

Hailey tuned out their conversation. Paige had been dreaming of working at an aquarium since they were kids. "What happened at the office to keep you and Trent late?"

"A hiccup with one of our programs. Everything is under control. You're getting better at catching the ball."

Clearly he didn't want to talk about work. "Thanks. I'm trying. What I really need to do is get better at batting."

"How about we go to the batting cages? I'm free tomorrow night."

"You're free on a Friday night? No hot date?"

He shot her a look of annoyance.

"Sorry. I'm having a hard time figuring us out. What's okay and what's not okay to say?"

"Good question. We are in an odd situation all things considered."

"For sure." Relief flowed through her like a rushing stream. "I'm glad I'm not the only one who thinks so." This tightrope they constantly had to balance on wobbled a lot. Talk about exhausting.

"Tell you what, let's be friends outside of work and almost equals at the office."

"I can live with that." He'd set the boundaries, and she would stay inside them.

Michael watched for Hailey's reaction to his suggestion. But her look was too guarded. He hated that he couldn't tell Hailey how he really felt. The last thing he wanted was to be just friends. She occupied his thoughts way too much. "Did you have dinner, Hailey?"

"I grabbed a bite on my way over with Paige." She stopped beside a car that had to belong to Paige since Hailey didn't own one.

"Okay. I'll see you in the morning." He moved to his car and got in then put the windows down, awaiting Trent.

The passenger door opened. "Sorry to keep you waiting. Paige is something else."

"You ask her out yet?"

"No. I've got too much going on right now. If I'm going to date someone I want to have the time and emotional energy to give to the relationship."

"Who said anything about a relationship? We're talking about one date."

"Says the man who is pining after his VP and refuses to do anything about it."

Michael put the car in gear and headed home. "You

know as well as I do, if something were to develop between us now, the office gossip would get out of control. If it wasn't for Ian keeping everyone in check regarding Hailey, who knows what kind of rumors would be flying."

"Yeah, I've heard some rumblings myself and had to set them straight."

"Who?"

"Savannah and Bree." Their office receptionist had a penchant for gossip.

"What was Bree doing in the office?"

"She's friends with Savannah, and they met for lunch."

"I don't like that." What if Savannah was telling Bree things that could help their competitors? If she valued her job she would keep her mouth closed since she had a confidentiality agreement like all the other employees at MM Enterprises.

"You can't control who our employees' friends are."

"I know." He gripped the steering wheel tighter. It had become more difficult to trust after what Mason did. Not everyone was out to steal from him and deceive him, but right now he was somewhat paranoid. He needed to move past that. But how, when his own cousin had almost ruined him?

"What's going on in that head of yours?" Trent had a way of knowing when something was up with him.

"Nothing."

"Right. It's me. I know you better than anyone."

Michael sighed. "I guess now that the immediate

crisis with the company is past, I'm out of panic mode, and I'm angry. I'm angry I was duped. I'm angry my own cousin stole from me. I'm angry I was put in a position where I saw no other option but to promote Hailey before she was ready. I'm just plain angry."

Trent blew out a breath. "Wow. I didn't see that coming. I thought you were conflicted about Hailey or worried about the game on Saturday."

"If only." No, his issues ran much deeper. "I'm telling you, Trent, if it wasn't for you, I think I would lose it."

"I guess that means you're no longer angry with me for not alerting you to my suspicion before I went to Europe."

"I got over that. Besides, you did me a favor. I might have done something I'd regret while you were away."

"Aw. You need me. I love you, bro."

Michael grinned as he pulled into their driveway. "I don't need you, but I am sure thankful you're around."

"That's right, I forgot you don't require anyone."

Michael got out. His brother's sarcasm was deserved. He hated admitting he could use help. The truth was he needed his brother and Hailey. They kept him grounded, even if Hailey was in over her head. Did she know? Somehow he had to find a way to help her. The last thing he needed was for her to quit. Then again, with the contract signed and the project moving forward, there was nothing Mrs. Morris could do if Hailey quit.

Trent stood on the porch watching him.

"What?" Michael stopped and looked up at him.

"I'm sorry."

"You have nothing to be sorry for." He headed up to the porch and pulled open the screen door.

"You going to be okay?"

"I will be." He pushed the door open, and they went inside. "You don't have any big trips planned, do you?"

"Not for a couple of weeks. Why?"

"I'd like for you to help Hailey understand what Mason did."

"I thought you went over all of that with her?"

"I did, but it didn't stick. If she had done her job right, we wouldn't have been late to practice."

"True, but she's still learning. You can't expect her to know it all."

Michael sighed. "I know you're right, but it doesn't help. The program did what it was designed to do. If Hailey had understood the client's needs to begin with we wouldn't be having this conversation." Maybe he should take on more of Mason's responsibilities. But if he did, then he'd be working sixty-hour weeks, and he promised himself when they opened the business he wouldn't let it take over his life. So much for that—it had taken over some time ago. But at least he still had a life. Things were about to change.

14

Hailey sat at her office desk with her head in her hands. She could do this, but oh how she wished she didn't have to. As it turned out, she'd provided the wrong information to the programmers, which had caused them to miss a crucial item the client wanted. She needed to talk with Michael about having one of their software developers meet directly with their clients. Cutting out the middleman, in this case—her—,would solve a lot of hassle for everyone. It wasn't an issue when Mason had been here, since he was a software developer, but she was clueless. She reached for the phone—time to call and make things right.

A rap on her door sounded and then either Michael or Trent walked in. It would be nice if they'd wear their hair differently. She glanced toward Michael's office—empty. "Michael?"

"Good morning. Have you made that call yet?"

"I was about to."

"Then I'm not too late. I already took care of the

situation. I'll be taking over that account as well as all the others except for the Morris project."

The tension in her shoulders eased. "Okay, but why?" Had she messed up so badly he'd lost faith in her?

"I'm going to shift some of my duties to you that I think are more suited to your skill set. I know you've worked a lot of overtime already, but if you have the time now, I'd like to train you on how to take over some of my responsibilities."

"I can give you an hour." She had a lot on her agenda today, but dealing with their disgruntled client had been her top priority. Now that Michael had saved her the task, she had time.

"That works." He pointed to her computer. "May I?"

She stood and stepped aside, curious what he was going to do. About ten minutes into his demonstration, she grabbed a pad and pen to take notes and pulled up a chair beside him. His aftershave had a clean scent—nice. Startled by the direction of her thoughts she yanked herself back to Michael's words.

"Any questions yet?"

"No." She looked at his profile as he continued on. His dark hair curled at his shirt collar. He needed a trim, but she didn't mind. What would his hair feel like?

"Hailey?" Michael's brows drew into a frown. "Is something on my neck?"

"What? No sorry. Go on."

"Maybe we should take a break. This is a lot to take in. Do you have any time after lunch?"

She had her schedule memorized. "My day is packed."

"I really need to go over this with you today. Do you have plans for after work?"

She shook her head. Other than playing catch with Paige, her evening was open. She'd text Paige and let her know.

"If you don't mind staying, I'll grab us a pizza, and we can plow through the bulk of this."

"Sure. That's fine." Somehow she'd manage to absorb the information after a long day.

"Great." He stood and left.

Hailey let out a breath. Working in such close quarters with Michael while hiding her growing attraction was not easy. Maybe she should find another job after all. Then they'd be free to pursue their attraction to one another. At least she thought he was attracted to her. Why else would he offer to help her with her batting skills on a Friday night?

The day whizzed by, and before it seemed possible, the office buzz had quieted to silence. Michael strode into her office carrying a pizza box and a plain brown bag.

"I come bearing sustenance. Let's eat first then get to work. I think better on a full stomach."

"Me too. The pizza smells delicious. What's in the bag?"

He placed the box on the corner of her desk then opened the bag and pulled out plates, napkins, and several bottles of soda as well as water. "I didn't know what you like, so I bought one of everything."

"Water is my usual drink of choice, but that root beer is calling to me."

He handed her the soda, along with a bottle of water. "For later."

"Thanks." She raised the lid on the box and a tingle of joy shot through her. "Half cheese half Canadian bacon and pineapple. Yum! I feel like I'm ten again."

He chuckled. "I would've thought you'd become well acquainted with pizza in college."

"Probably too well, but I tried to be healthy too and always got veggies on top."

He made a face. "That's criminal. Vegetables do not belong on pizza."

"It tasted good." She reached for a piece of cheese pizza and took a big bite. Her eyes watered from pure bliss.

"Are you crying?"

"I can't help it. This brings back so many memories of happy times. I think my mom used to get our pizza from this same place. It tastes exactly like I remember."

He shook his head. "I never asked. How did things go with your mom when she learned you're back?"

"Not well. Clearly I hurt her feelings by leaving, but to be honest I think my leaving was best for both of us. She got into counseling and seems to be doing much better. She's caustic toward me, but I have hope her attitude will turn around with time."

"I'm sorry she didn't welcome you home with open arms."

"Ha. That's not my mom's way. No, I'll have to earn my way back into her life." She focused on her pizza and took another mouth-watering bite. Oh, this was good.

Michael watched Hailey delight in the meal, taken aback at her emotional response. It was only pizza, but clearly it touched a strong memory. While her eyes were closed, he studied her. Her classic beauty and perfectly shaped nose nearly took his breath away. His stomach hitched as her eyes opened and locked on his gaze.

"Do I have sauce on my face?" She reached up and wiped her cheek with the back of her hand.

"You're fine."

"You were staring." Her eyes shifted, looking past his shoulder.

He knew there was nothing behind him since he faced the opposite wall that had no windows or doors. He rubbed the back of his neck. "Yes, just like you were earlier today." He took a breath and let it out. "This is nuts."

"What?" Her hazel eyes bore into him, begging him to stop, but this needed to be said.

"You and me—this thing between us. I don't know what to do about it. I'm attracted to you but…"

"But you have a rule. No office romances. So what do we do?"

"I don't know. I'm the boss. I make the rules, yet I

feel stuck. I don't want to do anything that will cause the staff to question why you were promoted to VP so fast. People talk."

"They should mind their own business."

"Agreed. But people will be people, and you can't stop their curiosity."

A sly look slid onto her face. "What if we hold a staff meeting and tell them exactly what's going on between us?"

He placed the back of his hand on her forehead. "Nope, cool as a cucumber. I thought for a moment you were delirious with fever after a statement like that."

She pushed his hand away, but he caught her wrist in his. "I'm serious. The truth will set you free. It says so in the Bible."

"Yeah, but you're taking that out of context."

She shrugged. "It still applies. We tell them exactly what's going on, then they will have nothing to gossip about."

"Your idealism is admirable, but I have strong doubts. What exactly would we tell them? We are attracted to each other, but we aren't dating?"

She frowned. "When you put it like that, it sounds like a ridiculous idea. I thought you wanted...oh never mind. You ready to work?"

"Not yet." They needed to clear the tension from the room. "We would have something to tell them if we start dating."

A slow grin spread on her face. "Are you asking me out? On a real date?"

"Yes. Are you free Saturday?"

"As it happens I have a softball game that day. What'd you have in mind?"

"I need to work on that part."

"How will I know what to wear?"

"It's Seattle."

She chuckled. "Good point. But if you take me someplace fancy, you better warn me. I don't want to be turned away or embarrassed because of a dress code."

"Promise. Now, let's get to work. I have a lot to teach you and not much time." His heart warmed at the look of joy on her face—he'd caused that. He wanted to do it more often.

At seven-thirty he pushed back from her desk. "Let's call it a night. We're both tired."

She closed the notepad she'd been writing in and stood. "My brain feels like it's been cramming for finals."

"How'd you do on finals when you crammed?"

"I aced them."

"That bodes well for me." He gathered up their garbage and noted they'd wiped out the pizza. "I'll give you a ride home."

"Thanks. I should buy a car, but I really like not having a car payment."

"There's something to be said for living debt free."

"For sure. Even though my mom was miffed at me for transferring to Chicago, she still paid my school bill, so I don't have a college loan to worry about either."

"Lucky lady. I just finished paying off mine. I celebrated by buying my new car."

"So you swapped one payment for another."

"Pretty much." He dumped the box and their garbage in the trash then piled the remaining soda back into the bag. He'd store them in his office mini fridge tomorrow. For now he tucked the bag right inside his office door. "You ready?"

She stood in her doorway with a messenger bag hanging from her shoulder and weary-looking eyes. "Yep."

"You look wiped out."

"Thanks a lot."

He chuckled and placed a hand on the small of her back as they navigated through the hall toward the exit. "Sorry. I didn't mean to be insulting. You look beautiful as always, but tired. Better?"

She tilted her head his direction. "You think I'm beautiful?"

Their steps slowed near the exit. "Absolutely." Her full lips drew him to her. Without thinking he brushed a kiss across her mouth. Awareness shot through him. He wanted more but pulled back.

Shock covered her face.

"Sorry. I shouldn't have done that."

"Maybe not, but I'm glad you did." She pulled open the door and looked over her shoulder. "You coming?"

He grinned. "Right behind you." They were playing with fire. The trick would be to avoid getting burned. The elevator door slid open, and they stepped inside.

Hailey turned to him. "You mentioned earlier that people had been talking. What were they saying?"

"Use your imagination. You're a beautiful woman with a brain to match. In less than two weeks of being at MM you were promoted to VP. What do you think they were saying?"

Her face blossomed a pretty shade of pink. "That's infuriating and embarrassing."

"It was dealt with, but now you see my hesitation to lay our relationship out for them?"

"You don't think they'll believe us?"

He shook his head. He had no doubt they'd create a storm of speculation. "Are you sure this is what you want?"

They stepped off the elevator in the lobby. "To date you and see where things go? Yes. To put myself out there for the staff to tromp on? Not so much."

He felt the exact same way. If there was some way to protect Hailey from what was to come if they went through with her plan, he'd do it. If only people would mind their own business and not invent salacious gossip he wouldn't be worried. As it stood now, he was deeply concerned for Hailey's reputation with the staff. She didn't need this right at the start of her career.

15

Saturday afternoon Hailey stood in her apartment facing her wardrobe with Katie on one side of her and Paige on the other. She needed to choose an outfit for her date tonight with Michael. He told her at the game this morning he'd made reservations for a dinner cruise.

Katie reached for a nice pair of jeans. "How about these?"

"Those could work. I was going for a little dressier though."

"You can dress up the outfit with your top and accessories," Paige said.

"Listen to you. When did you become a fashionista?"

"I pay attention to fashion tips when I see them on TV or in magazines." Paige reached for a sleeveless black top. "How about this?"

"Maybe. I wish I had time to go shopping for something new."

Katie checked her watch. "You have a few hours. There's time. It could be fun."

"It would be if my date wasn't in three hours. Besides, I already bought shoes this month. I need to control my spending."

Katie shook her head. "You and your brother are so much alike—very fiscally responsible."

"Thanks. I'll take that as a compliment."

"As you should." Katie pulled out a silky white top and a red one. "Why not try all of them? See which one best fits your mood."

For the next twenty minutes she tried on several different outfits, including a few Katie and Paige hadn't suggested. She finally settled on the jeans with the off-the-shoulder red top. She'd bring along a sweater if it was too cool.

"Anyone thirsty?"

"Yes." Katie and Paige said in unison.

"Me too. This warm weather makes me thirsty." She strolled over to the kitchenette and pulled open the fridge. "I have lemonade, water, and iced tea." She reached for the water, knowing Katie would want it, plus it sounded good to her too.

"Water for me," Paige said.

"Me too." Katie pulled open a cupboard and took out three glasses. "Everything is still exactly the way it was when I lived here. How come you haven't made it your own?"

"No time," Hailey said. "Besides, my goal is to live in a condo on the Sound or a lake."

"You want to live the dream." Katie stepped aside giving her space to pour the drinks.

"You got it. And Paige is going to room with me as soon as I can save enough money."

Katie frowned. "I know we don't spend much time together, but we'll miss you when you're gone."

"I won't be far. Besides, that's the distant future. I need at least six months before I'll feel comfortable moving out on my own."

"Good." Katie hugged Hailey then handed a glass to Paige. Katie's phone chimed a text message. She sighed. "Ray and the kids need me."

"Okay. Thanks for the help." Her sister-in-law was turning into a friend, and Hailey couldn't be happier. As Katie let herself out, Hailey turned to Paige. "You didn't mind Katie being here, did you?"

"Of course not. Do you want me to do your hair?"

"I thought I'd wear it down."

"Nothing fancy?" Paige's face fell.

Hailey giggled. "I'm going to wash it and blow it out."

"That could be nice."

Hailey playfully fluffed her hair. "Speaking of nice, I noticed you talking with Trent after the game today."

"Yeah. He wanted to see about practicing this next week. I told him I'd need to check with you."

"Michael mentioned something about that too." She padded into the bathroom to prepare for her date, although he probably wouldn't care if she did her hair or not. The man had seen her at her best and worst and wasn't scared off. Last night they'd gone to the batting cages. She'd actually left feeling confident she'd be able to hit the ball in a game. As it happened though, a live, unpredictable ball was much harder to make contact with than one that went to the same spot every time. At least she'd hit the ball once.

An hour later, she left the powder room smelling of fresh soap and sporting a blowout that would make Katie's hairdresser mother proud. Her jeans fit perfectly and the off-the-shoulder top was just right. She froze as she took in her living space then turned to Paige. "You cleaned my apartment." It even smelled clean. "Thank you! Wow. No one has ever voluntarily cleaned for me before."

"I was bored." Paige tossed a rag into the laundry then turned and looked her way. "Stunning. Guess now I know why you took forever in there."

"Thanks. He'll be here in about thirty minutes. You're sure I look okay?"

"Fishing for another compliment?" Paige teased. "You always look nice even covered in ball field dust. Want me to stay or go?"

"I like the company, but you probably shouldn't be here when he arrives."

"Then I'll leave now in case he shows up early. Have fun tonight and remember to be yourself. He already likes you for you. There's no need to try to impress him."

Hailey resisted rolling her eyes and walked her friend to the door. "You are the best friend a girl could ever have. Thanks for everything today." She gave Paige a rare hug. "I'll call tomorrow, so don't wait up for a report."

Paige frowned. "You're going to make me wait? After all I did?"

Hailey grinned. "Fine. I'll call." She waited until Paige headed for the stairs then closed the door and faced her sparkling clean apartment. Now what? She had absolutely nothing to do. She meandered over to her couch and sat staring at the far wall. When was the last time she had time to just be still? *Lord, thank you for my friends and family, including my mom. Please continue to heal that relationship, and please be with me tonight. I really like Michael, and I don't want to do anything stupid. Thanks.*

Michael sat across from Hailey at their private window table as they cruised Lake Union. Their first course had been cleared, and the second was being served. Hailey gazed out the window. She oozed happiness. He liked seeing this relaxed carefree side rather than the businesswoman or frustrated softball player he usually encountered.

"This is my first dinner cruise. I've been missing out." She smiled. "Thanks. I have a feeling we were lucky to book our spot at such late notice."

"That's what I was told. I'm glad you're having fun." Even though she was clearly enjoying herself, she'd been on the quiet side since he'd picked her up. They'd never actually spent time together outside of work related things—sans the train—so maybe that was the problem. They had nothing to talk about. "It occurred to me that you don't know much about me."

Her eyes widened. "Only what I've found on the Internet."

Their waiter served a salad for the second course.

"So nothing personal." He was careful about posting online and didn't even have a Facebook page other than the company page. "As you know, I have a twin brother. We've always been close. It's safe to say he's my best friend. I don't know what I'd do without him."

She nodded, encouraging him to go on.

"Our parents raised us to go to church. Are you a Christian?"

"I am, although I need to get back into the habit of going to church. It's been a while. When I went away to college, it was easier to sleep in on Sundays and watch a live-stream from my church here. I went with my brother's family last week."

"I'm glad you have Ray. He's a good man." He loaded his fork and ate a bite of the colorful salad. A burst of flavor filled his mouth.

"He's the best. So what else don't I know about you?"

"I like to run as much as I like to veg."

She laughed. "You're a study in contradictions."

Her smile and her melodious laugh were contagious.

The cruise and dinner flew by and before it seemed possible, they'd docked and were on their way back to Hailey's place. "I had fun tonight."

"You sound surprised."

"I wasn't sure. We'd never spent any time together outside of work."

"Not true. I distinctly remember swinging a bat with you last night, and I have the sore hands to prove it."

He'd get her batting gloves for next time. "Technically, that was business since it's office related. I was helping you prepare for our work-league game."

"Semantics."

He glanced her way as they drove by a lamppost that shined on her. Did she just roll her eyes? "Next time I want to take you to this food truck a couple blocks from my house. Frank makes the best gyros."

"Yum. I might have to take up running too with all this amazing food you're feeding me."

He couldn't stop smiling. Tonight had gone better than he'd hoped. "Assuming you want to go out again, let's keep that we're dating quiet for now at the office."

"I would like to continue dating, but why keep it quiet?"

"There's no need to stir things up right now." If they got serious, they'd figure it out together, but for now he wanted this between them. He valued his privacy and would hang onto it as long as possible.

"I suppose." She didn't sound convinced.

He pulled into her driveway and killed the engine. "May I walk you to your door?"

"I can manage on my own. Thanks for a nice night."

He grasped her hand. "Don't leave upset."

"I'm not upset. I'm confused."

"Because I want to wait before telling everyone at the office we're dating?"

The soft glow of the outside lights illuminated her just enough to see the pain on her face. "What changed? Have you decided you don't want to date me after all?"

Now he understood. "The opposite. I enjoyed tonight so much. I selfishly wanted to keep us quiet. I don't want anyone spoiling what we've started."

A slow smile spread on her face. "Oh."

"Are we okay?" He held his breath.

"Better than." She leaned toward him and placed a soft kiss on his lips.

He drew her closer and deepened the kiss, unwilling to settle for a brush of the lips this time. Her soft mouth responded to his, sending sparks shooting through him. He ran his hand through her silky hair, resting his forehead against hers. "Goodnight, Hailey," he said softly.

"I'll see you Monday," she whispered.

"Want to do something tomorrow? Monday is too long to wait."

She chuckled. "You realize Monday is the day after tomorrow."

"I'm not dim. Simply smitten."

"Hmm. Well, I think I can work you into my schedule. I'm going to church with my family then brunch with my mom—it's a set thing. Maybe tomorrow afternoon?"

"I'll call you." There was no way he'd be able to top the evening they'd had, but he wanted to spend time getting to know Hailey, the person, rather than Hailey, the professional. He'd had a glimpse of her personality on the train ride from Chicago, but she'd sealed that off as soon as they'd had the "talk."

"Okay. I'm leaving for real this time."

He released her hand and watched until she was safely inside her apartment. What had come over him this evening? He was always in control and sure of himself, but tonight he felt anything but.

16

Sunday brunch could possibly be the death of Hailey. Why did she think things had improved with her mother?

"I forbid you to see your boss again. It's unseemly." Mom placed her water goblet onto the table with a little more force than necessary, as if to punctuate her declaration.

Hailey's brain scrambled. She looked to Ray who offered nothing. She took a breath and let it out slowly. "I'm sorry you feel that way. However, I'm an adult, and I'll be making my own decision about who I will or will not date."

"It's a mistake. I know how this will end."

Anger surged through her. "How can you possibly know the future? You're not God."

"You're lucky I'm not."

"The world is lucky, because we'd all be your puppets. We at least have free will with Him in charge."

Her mother huffed. "When did you become so

impertinent? I raised you better than that. This is what I get for paying for your college education. Insolence."

"I don't mean to disrespect you, Mom, but I'm an adult, and I'm making an adult decision for myself. I did not ask for your permission, nor did I seek out your advice. I thought we were having a friendly conversation. I won't tell you about my life if it will only upset you."

"No. I want to know what's going on with you."

"Then please don't get upset and demanding when you disagree with how I'm living my life." She had so much more she wanted to say but hesitated. The ticking clock sounded like a time bomb in the silent room.

Mom pushed back from the table. "I think we're done here. You can see yourselves out." She walked from the room with her head high and shoulders back.

Hailey whirled to face Ray. "Thanks for the support, big brother."

He raised his hands. "Don't jump all over me. You didn't need my help. You handled that very well."

"Then why did she storm off in her dramatic way and basically kick us out?"

"Because that's who she is. Unless you plan to cave to her will, then you might as well get used to her drama."

She blew her breath out in a puff and crossed her arms.

Ray chuckled as he pushed back from the table. "She didn't uninvite us to brunch next week, so you can't have upset her too much."

"Good point. I didn't think of that." Then again,

being uninvited would have been nice. No, that wasn't entirely true. She wanted to restore her relationship with her mother and that required time and effort, plus a lot of prayer, because a miracle was needed where her mom was concerned.

"Let's clear the dishes and load the dishwasher."

"You don't think she'll mind?"

"You seem to have a selective memory. Mom always expects us to do the dishes."

"But she said to leave."

"Yep. After we do the dishes went without saying."

How was it her brother knew this and she didn't? She needed to pay more attention. She and Ray cleared the table then took care of the dishes.

Hailey spotted their mom out in her garden. "Should we say goodbye?"

"If you'd like. I'll be waiting in the car."

"Chicken?"

"This is between you and Mom, and I don't want to get in the way."

"Oh." She draped the dishcloth so it would dry then headed out back. Mom didn't appear to notice she stood only a yard away. She cleared her throat. "Ray and I are leaving now. The dishes are done. We'll see you next week."

"Fine."

Hailey crossed her arms. "Is this how it will always be between us? I know we've never had a cozy mother-daughter relationship, but you didn't used to be cold toward me. Am I wasting my energy here?"

Her mother stopped moving and stared forward with her back still to Hailey. "Good bye, Hailey."

Hailey's jaw dropped. Rather than go through the house she took a left through the garden gate. *Lord, I don't know what to do. Please give me wisdom, and please work on my mom too.*

She got into Ray's SUV and buckled up.

"How'd it go?"

"I don't want to talk about it."

"Now you sound like her."

Hailey glared at her brother then sighed and relaxed into the plush seat. "I'm sorry. I didn't mean to snap. It didn't go well. I probably should have followed your example and left without saying goodbye. At least then I wouldn't have made things worse."

"How did that happen?" He sounded surprised.

"I let my temper run away with my mouth."

"If it helps to know, Katie and I pray for Mom every day that her heart will be healed. She's a bitter and angry woman."

"With good reason. No mother should ever lose a child, even an adult child. But that's no excuse to treat the ones still living poorly."

"True. It's funny with Mom. She seems to be doing better, then she will backslide to her old ways. I suppose a lifetime of expecting the world to bend at her whim is a hard expectation to toss aside. She's accustomed to people meeting her demands."

"I've noticed." She'd seen the same quality in a couple of her parents' friends growing up and attributed it to their wealth. It seemed to her that money sometimes gave people a sense of entitlement, and in a sense that was her mom's issue. She felt entitled to rule over her family and when they didn't bend, she had a fit. Hailey prayed she never behaved like that. Everyone deserved to live their own life as they chose.

"Ray?"

"Um-hmm?"

"If I ever start to act like Mom will you please tell me?"

"I promise."

"Thanks. I love her, but right now I don't like her very much, and I want to give up on trying to fix things with her."

"Maybe you should."

She whipped her head in his direction. "Why do you say that?"

"She knows you're trying, and it's a game with her. As long as you are pursuing her, she's in control."

"Oh my. I didn't think of that, but you're right. What should I do?"

"Don't try so hard. Show up at our brunch and let her talk. You listen."

"Like you did today?"

"Exactly. If she asks a question, choose your words wisely. Keep to safe topics like the weather."

She laughed. "Seriously?"

"Yes. It's worked for me for years. Try it."

"I will. Thanks." She looked out the passenger

window as they drew closer to Ray's driveway. "In case you didn't know, I love you, Ray."

"Love you too, Grace."

She wrinkled her nose. "You had to go and ruin the moment with that ridiculous nickname. I thought I'd outgrown it."

He chuckled as he pulled into the driveway. "Enjoy the rest of your day, Grace." He got out and laughed all the way to the house.

"Whatever." Clearly her brother needed a stress reliever. In truth, she only pretended to hate the nickname she'd received as a kid because she'd been the opposite of graceful. She secretly enjoyed their banter whenever he called her Grace. Her phone rang. She answered.

"Hi, Hailey. It's Michael."

She grinned as she got out and climbed the stairs to her apartment. "Hey, there. Do you still want to do something today?"

"I do, but I forgot about this thing with Trent. I need to cancel."

Disappointment filled her. She kept her tone upbeat. "It's fine. Is everything okay?"

"Fine. This has been on our calendar for a long time. I spaced it."

"Okay. See you tomorrow." She never should have gotten out of bed today. Aside from church, this day had stunk.

Monday morning, Michael strode through the door leading from the parking garage to the lobby of his office building. Hailey stood outside on the sidewalk talking to some dude. He paused and took a closer look. His body heated, and he clenched a fist. What was she doing talking with their biggest rival? He marched to the doors and stepped outside. "Hailey?"

"Oh hi, Michael. Have you met Tom? He owns a start-up—"

"We're acquainted." He nodded to Tom then looked to Hailey. "You ready to head up?"

"Sure. I'll see you around, Tom." She walked inside with Michael. "Is everything okay? You seem a little uptight."

"Why were you talking with Tom?"

"Savannah introduced us."

"He was in the office?"

"Yes, he and Savannah are seeing each other."

He ran a hand over his face. How had he not known this? "What was he saying to you?"

"What's with all the questions? You have nothing to be jealous about."

The elevator doors opened, and they went inside. "I'm not jealous. I don't like the way Tom does business."

"Okay. Are you sure that's all that's bothering you? Did everything go okay with Trent yesterday?"

"Yes and yes." The doors slid open and they got off. He held the door to the office for her. "After you."

"Thanks."

Fortunately, the only person to witness their arrival was Savannah. He needed to make it clear she had a confidentiality agreement and couldn't talk about work details to anyone outside the office. "Savannah, please meet me in my office in five minutes. I'd like to talk to you before things get busy." Without waiting for a response he strode to his office.

Hailey followed him. "Want me to sit in on your meeting with Savannah?"

"Great idea. And please record it. I don't want this conversation to come back and sting me."

Hailey's eyes widened before she left and went into her office. Today was definitely Monday.

Twenty minutes later, Savannah left his office with red-rimmed-eyes. "I'd hoped that would go better."

Hailey sat in the chair for guests. Her arms were crossed, and she wasn't smiling. "You act like everyone is out to get you. Not everyone is like Mason."

"I know."

"Then what's the deal? You have some serious trust issues regarding the employees here."

He sucked in a sharp breath. What did she know? She had a great life with a supportive brother. She didn't have to pay her way through college like he had. Everything had been handed to her—including her current job. She had no idea what it was like to struggle to get what she wanted. He wasn't born with a silver spoon in his mouth like Hailey. He understood hard work.

"There's no way you can possibly understand."

"Try me." Hailey raised her chin.

Why did she have to be so adorable when she was angry? He averted his gaze. "I worked my way through college and then worked even harder to get this business up and running. It's very personal with me. I wasn't born into money. I've had to work for everything I have."

"And I haven't?"

He raised a brow. Did she seriously think she'd worked her way into her current position? "No. I don't believe you have. You've been blessed." He kept his voice low, hoping to diffuse the anger that shot from her.

"I can't argue with that, but just because I've had some things come easier for me doesn't mean I haven't worked hard to get where I'm at."

"I'll concede you're a hard worker. I've not witnessed anyone as devoted to helping this company succeed as you've been, and I appreciate it more than you can imagine."

"But?"

"Nothing."

"Fine. In the future, you might not want to tell your employees who they can and can't socialize with."

"I didn't." *Had he?*

"Maybe not those exact words, but it was implied that if she continued seeing Tom, her job was in jeopardy. You can't control who your employees date or who they hang out with." She shook her head. "You remind me of my mom. I wish I'd realized you were a control freak." She stood and strode from the office.

He stood to follow then caught himself. She needed space, and he could use some too. What did she mean he reminded her of her mom? Whatever it was, it wasn't good and that hurt. A similar conversation he'd had with Trent echoed in his mind. He'd said virtually the same thing about being controlling.

Trent strode into his office. "What's going on? Savannah about bit my head off when I wished her good morning."

Michael sighed. "Close the door." He told his brother the entire sordid story in detail then waited.

"You need a vacation. This thing with Mason has messed you up."

"Maybe so, but I can't take a vacation right now. Since Mason is out of the picture and this company is my sole responsibility, now is the worst possible time for me to check out."

"You have Hailey and me."

"Right. You really think she can run things here on her own? Because I don't. She's too young and lacks experience."

"What about me? I can fill your shoes."

"Literally, but not figuratively. Come on, Trent. You're the best, but there are things you've never had to handle."

"Then it'll keep. You need to get out of here, and I don't mean sulking at home. Get away. Go someplace and gain some perspective. Until you do, everything you touch is going to be clouded by your anger with Mason."

Michael blew out a breath. "Maybe you're right." He'd wanted to go to Vancouver, BC for a while. Maybe a few days away would do the trick. He could drive and be there in a few hours. "Okay. I need to go over some stuff with you, then I'll head home and pack."

Surprise filled Trent's eyes.

"What? You didn't think I would listen to reason?"

"Not for a second." He grinned.

Michael had a lot of making up to do if his best friend in the entire world had lost faith in him to do the right thing.

17

Hailey rang the bell beside the front door of her mother's house. Ever since her conversation with Michael this morning she'd determined to clear the air with her mother—it wasn't her mom's way, but doing things her way wasn't working.

The door opened slightly. "Hailey?" Mom opened the door wider. "Is everything okay?"

"No. It's not. We need to talk. Now."

Mom frowned and stepped aside. "I wish you would have called, I could have prepared dinner for you."

"Sorry, I came here on impulse and didn't think to call. Don't worry about feeding me. Did I interrupt your meal?"

Mom waved a hand before settling on an overstuffed chair in their formal living room. "I snack all day and don't eat real meals most of the time. What brings you by so unexpectedly?"

Hailey winced—another dig. "I'd like to clear the air between us."

"What are you talking about?"

"I'm talking about how we left things when I was here last and having to call before coming. I'm talking about you trying to control my life even though I'm twenty-four years old and the vice president of a company. I can take care of myself, Mom."

"Really? You call living above your brother's garage taking care of yourself."

"Yes, I do. He asked me to stay. It's an opportunity for me to live cheaply and build a savings so I can buy a place of my own."

"I suppose when you put it like that, it makes sense. You could have moved here and accomplished the same goal."

"I didn't think I was welcome. You were angry when I transferred to Chicago."

"I've been angry for years, but it's not about you."

"It feels that way."

Mom picked at an imaginary piece of lint on the arm of the chair. "I'm sorry. I'll try to not project my anger onto you. My therapist says I do that and that I need to tell you that I love you."

Hailey tensed. Her mom never said that. Ever. Come to think of it, technically she still hadn't.

"I tell you I love you, and I get silence?"

"You didn't say it."

She puffed out a breath. "I love you, Hailey. I know I don't show it and this might be the only time I ever say the words, but now you know."

A tingle shot through her. The words she'd wanted to hear for so long had finally been spoken. "I love you too." Her throat thickened and her eyes burned with unshed tears. She cleared her throat. "Are we okay then? You're not mad at me?"

"I was for a long while. That day you first showed up here with your brother I was thrilled to see you, but when I found out you weren't staying it was like a slap in the face. My anger was stoked, and I've let it flame frequently since. I'm sorry—my genius therapist pointed all of that out to me. I'm working on doing better."

"The gardening isn't helping?"

A small smile touched Mom's lips then grew. "I hate gardening. I only do it because it's all I could come up with besides crafting, knitting, or sewing to try as a hobby that would keep me at home. I don't want to see my friends' looks of pity. After your sister's death, I decided staying home was safer."

"But you go to your therapist's office?"

"Once a week, I go out to run errands and attend appointments."

"I didn't know."

"No reason you would have." Her mom stood. "Now that my secret is out, I'm going to hire a gardener. I like the fresh veggies, but I really hate getting dirt on my hands and in my fingernails."

Hailey chuckled softly. Now that sounded like the mom she remembered. "You glossed over one issue that I really need to resolve with you before I leave."

"What's that?"

"I need you to step back and let me be an adult. No more trying to control my life. And if you could stop the verbal jabs I would sure appreciate it."

"Fine. I'll do my best, but it won't be easy."

"I don't imagine it will be." Her eyes widened and her gaze shot to her mom's. "Sorry. I didn't mean that how it sounded."

Mom waved off the slight. "It's the truth and we both know it. Are we done?"

Hailey hesitated. Would Mom be able to help her with Michael? They'd never had a close relationship and never talked about boys, but it seemed like her mom might have a little wisdom in this. Then again, taking baby steps with her might be best.

"Out with it, Hailey. You are chewing on something so thick I can see it from here."

"You know Ian recommended me to my boss at MM Enterprises and that I was hired on as their economist?"

"I heard something about that."

"Well, my boss, Michael, is the person who came to Chicago to interview me. I assumed he was Michael's assistant. We clicked. He ended up on the same train home as me, and I found myself telling him things I never talk about. We have a connection."

"But he's your boss. When did you figure that part out?"

"At the end of our trip he came clean and told me in no uncertain terms that it's against company policy for us to date."

"So what's the problem?"

"The same week I started my job there was a huge

shift in the company. Michael bought out his partner and asked me to be his VP. I accepted, but now it has complicated things even more."

"How?"

"Well, we broke his rule and as you already know went out on a date Saturday."

"And now you're afraid if word gets out everyone will think you slept your way to your promotion. The exact reason I was against this from the start."

"Pretty much. But what's worse is Michael is a control freak. He got upset that I was talking with a man who is one of his competitors." She couldn't tell her mom about what happened with Savannah per her confidentiality agreement. "I thought since you both have control issues you might be able to offer some advice. I want to help him, but I really don't know how."

Mom's face reddened. "Who would've thought one of my biggest flaws is what got my daughter to ask for advice? I don't recall you ever doing that before."

Hailey shrugged. Her mom wasn't exactly a nurturer, so why would she?

"Unfortunately, I don't have any advice. You can't change who he is. Are you going to continue dating him?"

"I don't think so. I'm attracted to him, enjoy being with him, and I care a lot about him, but I can't be in a relationship with someone who wants to control me, so there's no point in going out with him again."

"I'm sorry. I imagine that was a difficult conclusion to come to."

"It was." She still wasn't sure it was what she wanted, but it made the most sense. "I should go. Thanks for listening."

"You bet. You're welcome to stop in anytime, Hailey, but a phone call first is always appreciated."

"Okay. I'll try and remember that. See you Sunday."

Would their Sunday brunches be better now? One thing she knew for sure, her mom was lonely. If only she knew how to help.

Michael gazed out the window of his waterfront hotel at the cruise ship that had recently docked and sipped his coffee. He had no plans for the day other than relaxing and getting his head straight—soul searching. He had chewed on his brother's and Hailey's words the entire drive up to Canada yesterday. He'd never thought of himself as a having a control problem but maybe he did. He didn't want to be like that and finally realized for him, trust was the root of the problem.

Mason had broken his trust, and he'd been burned a few times too many by others. It seemed that control was the natural response to being unable or unwilling to extend trust.

He turned away from the window, grabbed his Bible and sat in a chair facing the view. *Lord, I need help to work past this. I don't want to always feel the need to be in control. I don't want to be afraid to trust others. Please give me the wisdom to know when to trust and when to be cautious.*

He turned to Proverbs chapter three and began to read. Verses five and six leapt out at him. Trust in the Lord. *I trust in You.*

Then give me your fear.

Whoa. Was it really that simple? Well, not easy, but the Lord had never failed him. He'd provided Hailey right when they needed her. He'd given him a brother who understood numbers. At every challenge He'd provided the help Michael had needed. Maybe He didn't stop the bad stuff from happening, but He did help him deal with it.

It sure would be nice if He'd stop the garbage before it happened, but that wasn't how God worked. He let humanity have a free will—yes. He was always in control but He wasn't a control freak. Michael sucked in a breath. If the God of the universe wasn't a control freak what was he doing trying to control the people in his life? It wasn't his job or his purpose.

Michael set the Bible aside and stood. He needed to chew on this new awareness. And walking along the water seemed the perfect place to ponder. People strolled past, no one paying him any special interest. Voices from the docks filtered through the air. Life went on around him as if nothing was amiss. Clearly, he couldn't control everyone in his life, nor should he try. Perhaps going with the flow was a concept he needed to incorporate into this life.

He wasn't a go-with-the-flow kind of guy. Baby-steps would be key. He blew out a breath. With the Lord's help he knew he could do this.

18

Monday morning Michael slipped into the office extra early. He returned from Canada the night before after his soul-searching adventure. The trip would have been more fun with his brother or Hailey along, but that would have defeated the purpose.

For the first time since he learned of Mason's thievery his head was on straight. He sat behind his desk and booted up his computer. A knock on his door made him jump. He looked up. "Trent. You're in early."

"So are you. Is everything okay? You came in late last night, so we didn't get a chance to talk."

"Come in and have a seat. Better close the door in case someone else shows up early." Hailey had a habit of being early, and he didn't want her to overhear this conversation.

Trent closed the door then took a seat. "What's going on?"

"First of all, thank you for calling me out on my behavior and suggesting I get away." His brother's face didn't reveal his thoughts, but he knew Trent appreciated his words. "I was angry and afraid, which made me try to control everyone around me."

"Are you still angry?"

"Not so much. I spent time reading my Bible and talking with God. I realized He doesn't try to control us and that regardless of what happens here or in my personal life, He's with me and will help me through it if I let Him. I want Him in control, not me. I realized if He is in control then I can't be."

"Interesting. But you just said He doesn't try to control us."

"He wants us to choose to follow Him rather than be coerced or manipulated into it. If I choose to give Him control that's a lot different than Him taking it, like I was trying to do."

Trent nodded but remained silent.

"There will be some changes here from today forward. Starting with a lifting of the no fraternizing rule."

"Are you sure? There could potentially be a lot of drama in the office when people break up."

Michael shrugged. "I'm done being the social police."

"Okay. I'm going to hold you to that."

"Thank you. Now, how did things go while I was away?"

"Other than Savannah being furious with you, fine."

He winced. If he could take back what he'd said he would. Hopefully she'd settle for an apology. "Will you let me know when she arrives? I need to clear the air with her."

"Sure. So you're okay with everything now?"

He still needed to have a heart-to-heart with Hailey, but that would keep until after the staff meeting. "Pretty much. I need to send off an email to everyone about a staff meeting this morning. Will you also make sure the conference room is ready and order in some coffee and pastries?"

"What has come over you? You realize we are operating on a budget?"

"Sometimes it pays to boost morale. Please take care of it."

"Will do." Trent stood and left his office.

Michael set to work sending out an email to the staff about a meeting at ten this morning. He'd checked the master calendar and ten was the only time everyone would be in the office at the same time for any length of time.

Hailey entered her office a little before eight, but never looked his direction. His stomach sank. She always greeted him when she arrived, and he wasn't sitting in the dark, so she had to know he was back. It looked like he'd done more damage than he'd realized. He hoped today's staff meeting would fix everything, because short of seeking out her brother's help, he didn't know what else to do, except pray.

Lord, you know what's going on in Hailey's head. Please help her to hear my words today and forgive me.

Work had piled up while he was away so he got

busy. Two hours later he grabbed a water bottle and took a cleansing breath before heading to the conference room. All twelve staff members gathered around the table and were enjoying donuts and coffee. Some looked tense and others looked at ease. Interesting. It wasn't like he never had spontaneous meetings. But maybe word had gotten around about his conversation with Savannah last week.

He sat at the head of the table and everyone quieted. "Good morning. I'm pleased everyone could make it. I want to start off with telling you that you are all doing a great job."

A few faces relaxed.

"In fact I'm so impressed by your hard work and professionalism that I'm lifting the ban on intra-office fraternization."

A dull roar broke out.

"Hear me out, please. I realize we have few women working here, but that could change at any time as the company grows and expands. As you've no doubt noticed, there have been big changes with the leadership of MM Enterprises. I know change is seldom easy and often comes with challenges, but I hope you will agree that we've weathered this transitional time well."

Several people nodded, others had blank looks on their faces.

"I hope you will come to me or Hailey if you have any questions or concerns. We have an open door policy and want to be accessible to each of you." He glanced at

Hailey and noted surprise in her eyes before she hid it. "I know you're all busy, so I won't keep you any longer."

The staff stood and started to filter out. "Savannah, a word?"

Her shoulders slumped slightly.

"I meant to talk with you when you came in earlier today, but time got away from me. I want to apologize for what I said last week. I was upset about something else and took it out on you. You have my word that it will not happen again. Who you date and talk to is none of my business. I'm sorry. I trust you to keep what we do here confidential."

Savannah's eyes widened, and her lips tipped into a half smile. "I appreciate that. Thank you." She walked out with her head held high.

He blew his breath out and sank into the nearest chair.

Trent sat beside him. "You did good. The donuts and coffee were a nice touch too. When everyone saw the goodies the mood immediately shifted."

"Glad to hear it." He stood. "In case I haven't said it recently, thanks." He left and headed back to his office. He hesitated in the space between his office and Hailey's. She sat at her desk fully focused on something. He went to the doorway and heard her talking. He'd have to catch her later. She'd had a conference call meeting on her calendar, but he'd hoped to catch her before it started.

Hailey knocked on her brother's kitchen door.

Katie answered. "This is a happy surprise. Come in."

"Thanks. Are you busy?"

"No busier than normal. But the kids are all at their swimming lessons. So we have the house to ourselves. Would you like something to drink?"

"Ice water sounds good. Thanks." Hailey had come to see Ray, but there was no way she'd show Katie her disappointment.

Katie handed her a cold glass then sat at the kitchen table. "I'm glad you stopped by. I asked Ray to give you an invitation to Alex's birthday party for this coming weekend, but he keeps forgetting. It's Sunday afternoon. We invited your mom too. She declined."

"Her loss. I'll be there." It would be a full day between church, brunch and then a party, but that was okay. She wanted to be part of her nephew's life and birthday parties were a big deal. Besides that, it would keep her mind occupied and off work and Michael. She missed him.

"What's wrong, Hailey?" Concern filled Katie's eyes. "And don't say nothing."

"It's why I came over. I was hoping to talk shop with Ray."

"I know I'm not your brother, and I don't have the education the two of you have, but I'm a great sounding board. Maybe saying out loud what you're thinking will help."

She could have a point, but really what good would it do? She'd always trusted her big brother when it came to life decisions. And this was a big one. "You have to promise me this won't leave the kitchen. If word got out, I'd be sunk."

"I promise."

"I still can't believe this, but another software company is trying to get me to leave MM Enterprises. They have offered me an incentive package that's hard to say no to."

"Then why haven't you said yes?"

"Two reasons. The first is I think he only made the offer to get under Michael's skin. Second, I like MM Enterprises. Most of my co-workers are great, there's generally a good vibe there, and..." Michael had lifted the no fraternizing rule. But after what he'd said last week, could she go there with him? He'd definitely come back from his vacation a new man, but how long would it last?

"And?" Katie asked.

"And I think I'm falling in love with my boss. I don't want to hurt him even though I can't be with him."

"Whoa. You're in love with Michael?"

She nodded. It felt good to admit the truth. "But I don't see us working. He's too much like my mom. Everything needs to be his way, and he seems to take issue with the fact that I was raised in a well-to-do family."

"Hmm. I can understand all of those things. I'm somewhat of a control freak myself, but I've worked hard at letting go of some things."

"Ray's never said a word."

"I should hope not. The fact that Ray comes from money wasn't an issue for us, mostly because I didn't realize how well off he is. To say I was blind and naïve about Ray's professional life and upbringing would be accurate. Renee was never pretentious like your mom, who was a shock. I didn't expect her wrath on our wedding day."

Hailey pushed away the sadness that hit her at the reference to her older sister's name. At least she didn't get depressed, or feel like crying anymore at the mention of her name. "My mom even shocks me at times, but she's not as awful as she comes across."

"Seriously? I've never seen a redeeming quality in her."

"Ouch. I don't think that's fair." Even though she'd had some harsh thoughts about her mom she didn't want others to voice them. "You never knew her before Renee's accident. Sure she was pretentious and a snob toward some people, but her heart was generally in the right place."

"She definitely has a mama bear quality." Katie sipped her water.

"For sure. I'm sorry for getting riled up. I suppose I have that mama bear quality myself at times."

"I get it. She's your mom and no one but you or Ray can say a negative thing about her."

Laughter bubbled up from Hailey.

"What's so funny?" Katie traced the pattern of the wood table with her finger.

"Well, she's your mother-in-law. So she's fair game. I'm sorry for being defensive. If anyone understands what it's like to be on the receiving end of my mom's wrath it's me, and I suspect you too. So, I'm sorry for getting defensive. If you ever need to vent I'm here for you. After all, sisters should be there for each other."

Katie's hand stilled. "I've never had a sister."

"Well you do now."

Katie blinked back tears and stood then bent over and hugged Hailey. "Thank you." She backed away and wiped her face. "Our conversation took a turn. We never resolved your problem."

Hailey stood. "It's fine. Talking helped. Thanks." She left still unsure about her next move but relieved she wasn't carrying the burden alone. It felt good to tell someone about the offer.

19

Rambunctious children flitted here and there in the crowded pizza place. A frazzled parent pursued them while other adults looked on. This was the place to go for birthday parties, according to Katie. Alex turned four today, and all his little friends were there to celebrate with him. Emily sat beside her mom and little cousin and happily ate cupcakes in the booth seat across from Hailey, while Alex and his little buddies sat at a different table. Thankfully, the pizza place hosted the party and had done a great job keeping the kids entertained.

The parents would soon be back to take their little darlings home, and Hailey couldn't be more relieved. She loved her nieces and nephew and their little friends were fine, but two hours was long enough.

"Who's that man talking to Uncle Ray?" Emily asked.

Hailey turned in her seat to see Ray standing near the boys' table talking with Michael. She gasped and looked to her sister-in-law. "I didn't tell him I was here."

"He called to talk with Ray last night. He mentioned the party today, but I didn't know he planned to stop by."

"Who is he?" Emily asked again.

"He's my boss, sweetie. Please excuse me for a minute?" She stood and headed toward the men, dodging running children along the way.

Michael spotted her and his face lit, sending her stomach into a somersault. She hadn't talked one-on-one with him since the day they'd had words over him being controlling.

Ray turned right then. "I'll leave you to talk in private."

There wasn't anything private about this place. "I'm surprised to see you here," Hailey said. "Would you like a cupcake?"

"No thanks. Ray said the party is pretty much over. Do you mind taking a walk? I was hoping we could talk."

"Uh…sure. Let me say goodbye and grab my purse. I'll meet you at the door." She hustled back to her family. "He wants to talk."

"We can wait for you if you'd like," Ray said.

"No thanks. I'll manage."

"Okay. I'm only a phone call away if you need me."

How often had she heard a friend's parents say that? No one besides Ray had ever told her that. Overcome with love for her brother she gave him a hug—Katie must be rubbing off on her too. "You're the best big brother a girl could ask for." She went to the party table

175

and wished her nephew happy birthday once more then headed toward the exit where Michael stood, fitting right in with his casual attire of khakis and T-shirt with an unbuttoned shirt layered over top.

He opened the door wordlessly and walked toward the parking lot. "I told Ray I'd bring you home if you agreed."

"I'd appreciate that. I'm surprised to see you here."

"Yes. I tried to catch you at work this past week, but every time I approached you—."

"I bolted. I suppose that was childish of me. I'm sorry."

"It's okay. I understand why you avoided me. I spoke with your brother yesterday, and he mentioned you'd be at his son's birthday party."

"So you figured you'd show up there." She wasn't sure how she felt about that. Was he trying to control the situation by surprising her or was she reading too much into his actions? She glanced his way. He seemed nervous. She'd cut him some slack. "How was your vacation?"

He opened the door to his vehicle for her. "Enlightening."

"Tell me more."

"Well..." He grinned as he closed the door then went around and got situated in the driver's seat. He started the engine then pulled out. "I did a lot of soul searching. It was good to get away and leave work distractions behind. I've missed *you* though."

"Thanks. Same here. But I think it was good that

you went away. I've seen some positive changes in you since you've been back."

"I'm glad. I've been trying. How do you think things are going at the office?"

"Better." She still needed to tell him about her idea, but it would keep until the right moment. "Where are we going?"

"The park near my house."

"Sounds good. I'm glad you stopped by. I wanted to talk with you also."

"What about?"

"Us." She'd done some soul searching as well.

"I like that topic." He maneuvered through Sunday afternoon traffic.

"You might not like what I have to say."

His grip tightened on the steering wheel. "Then maybe I could go first?" He glanced her direction.

She nodded.

He cleared his throat. "While I was in Canada I came to realize that I was allowing fear to dictate how I approached life and those in my life. I also realized I dealt with that fear by trying to control everything and everyone. I don't want to do that anymore."

"Good for you." Sincerity filled her voice. "That puts the staff meeting into perspective. What else are you doing to fulfill that goal? Wanting to do something and doing it aren't the same."

He chuckled. "That was direct. But you're correct."

Should she apologize? No. There was nothing wrong with being direct.

"They say acknowledging a problem is the first step to fixing it."

"I've heard the same." She wished he'd spit it out already. She'd planned to cut it off with him, but now she needed to know what he had to say, and he was taking too long. Was there a chance they could still have a future together? Her stomach somersaulted at the thought.

He found a spot and parked. "I prayed and asked the Lord to take away my fear and to help me be okay with not always being in control. I also asked Trent to hold me accountable."

She nodded. "Those are both excellent ideas. How's it going so far?" She reached for the door handle and got out. The car was becoming hot.

"So far so good, but I need your help too."

He met her at the hood. "Mine?" He set out along the paved path.

She stayed by his side. "Yes. You see, I find the areas where I am most vulnerable are the ones where I am the most controlling."

Now she understood. "Do you need me to hold you accountable too?"

"Yes. Not only at work but outside as well. And you should know I apologized to Savannah. I realized how out of line I was. You were right to call me out on what I said."

Hailey had no idea how to respond. Every word he spoke changed where her head had been. This was a man she could support. That he humbled himself enough to share his heart with her drew her to him so strongly she had to resist the urge to loop her arm though his, like she'd done once before without thinking. She'd felt comfortable with him, as if they'd always known one another. Then after his confrontation with Savannah everything changed, but now things were changing again.

"I also realized that I put you in an impossible situation."

"What are you talking about?" She wrapped her arms around her middle as they walked along the paved path through the quiet park.

"I was so desperate to save my company I neglected to think about what was best for you professionally. I know that things have been…challenging."

"That's putting it mildly, but since you brought it up, I have a solution."

"What's that?" He stopped walking and faced her.

"Rather than have me in charge of meeting with clients about their needs, we should have a software developer do it. Someone good with people, who communicates well."

"We've done some shifting of responsibilities. I thought things were working better." He frowned.

"To some degree, yes. The thing is Mason is a software engineer. I'm not. It doesn't make sense for me to replace him in that role. We need someone like Ian to do that."

"Hmm." He grinned. "I see your point. Good idea. I should've thought of that myself."

"I'm sure you would've had you not been so

stressed from the mess Mason left you."

"Thanks. Would you like to ask Ian if he's up to the task or should I?" Michael asked.

"I'll do it. I imagine it'd mean he'd have to travel more, and he'd receive a raise right?"

"Yes, but not a big raise—at least not yet. We need to get things back on track first."

"Okay. I assume he can't know the company's financial situation."

"Correct."

She nodded and took a slow deep breath before letting it out. It was time to talk about them. As much as she wanted to be with him and as hopeful as she felt about a future with him, she couldn't do it—not yet. "I'm encouraged by everything you've said, but I still think you and I need to take a step back."

"Why?" Confusion filled his eyes.

"For starters it's too much for me right now."

"What's going on?"

She may as well tell him everything. "Your control issue really concerned me. I'm pleased to see how serious you're taking the problem, and more than anything I want there to be an us. But I realized as you were talking that I need to see the fruit of your labor before I let my heart become more entangled. There's something else."

"Why do I feel like I'm not going to like this?"

"Because you're a smart man." She took a breath and let it out slowly. "I was offered a position at one of your competitors. Their incentive package is unbelievable."

Michael's insides wilted. He'd hoped to win Hailey back today, not learn that someone else sought her too—well maybe not in the same way, but he didn't want to lose her professionally or personally. "What are you going to do?" He was almost afraid to hear her answer.

"After talking with you today, I realized my time at MM Enterprises isn't up yet. I like you and Trent and most everyone else there. If we can get Ian to take over dealing with our client's needs, then I'm all in."

Guarded relief filled him. "It sounds like you'd be giving up a lot to stay. You should know I couldn't offer you anything more than you're already getting."

"I don't expect you to. What I'm giving up is nothing compared with what I gain by sticking with you. I have a lot to learn, and I believe your company is the perfect place for me right now. Besides the perks here are pretty good."

"I'm happy to hear that."

She laughed. "I was kind of annoyed you crashed my nephew's party, but now I couldn't be happier. After thinking long and hard over it, I seriously considered taking the other offer before you came back from Canada, then the little changes I've been seeing in the office had me hesitating. Today sealed the deal."

He took her hand and gave it a squeeze. She slipped it away, then he remembered what she led with—she didn't want her heart entangled with his. Wait, she said *more* entangled—knowing she cared helped to soften his disappointment. "Sorry. I didn't mean to overstep."

"It's okay."

"So you're staying with the company, but you and I are over?"

She sucked in a sharp breath. "I don't like how that sounds, but I think it's for the best that we take a step back."

His insides twisted. This was not what he wanted, but he had to respect her decision. "Is there any hope for us down the road?" There had to be, based on what he'd heard her say, but yet, he couldn't be certain.

She shrugged. "I honestly don't know. I really care about you, but things are so messed up right now."

Forget it. He had to say his piece. "Life is messy, Hailey. There will always be challenges to overcome. Let's face those challenges together, both professionally and personally. I like who I am when I'm with you. You make me a better person and call me on my garbage."

She grinned. "Thank you, that was sweet."

"It's the truth." He had to make her see that they were better together than apart.

"I think facing the challenges together sounds nice. But I'm concerned about those times you want to control everything."

He rubbed the back of his neck then guided them over to a bench in the shade. "I can't promise to never try and control things, but I can promise if you point it out when I do, I'll do my best to adjust my approach."

"I need some time to think this through."

"Of course. Whatever you need." He wouldn't push her anymore lest she think he was trying to control her.

"Thank you. I appreciate that. Would you take me home now?"

He nodded. How would they get back to where they were before he lost his cool with Savannah?

Hailey sat on the floor in her brother's living room playing blocks with little Sophie while her brother and sister-in-law took the older kids for a bike ride. She placed a block on the top of their tower. "Tada."

Sophie clapped and danced in place then knocked the tower over. "Again." She squatted and started the base.

Hailey watched her sweet niece prepare the foundation. Even a toddler knew the importance of a strong foundation. Did she have that with Michael or even her mom? Her mind wandered to the day she'd met the man and how the caution reflected in his eyes gradually turned to acceptance then pleasure. Yes, they'd had an odd beginning, but their foundation was strong. He was right when he said there would always be challenges to overcome. She trusted him despite her concerns about his control issue—concerns that had faded substantially since her talk with him.

Her thoughts drifted to her mother. She'd been closer with her dad, but mostly because her mom didn't seem to know what to do with a child. She was not a hands-on parent like their dad had been. Mom preferred to hire a sitter or stick them in front of the television. Did they have a foundation that would stand the test of time? She'd like to think so. Mom might be self-centered, but she cared for her children. Of that there was no doubt. She'd created her own kind of foundation—though not ideal to Hailey's thinking, it was still based on love, and she knew that things were going to be okay where her mom was concerned.

Sophie patted Hailey's face with her chubby hands. "You play too."

"Sorry, sweetie." She placed a block on the second level. Her niece couldn't be more adorable. Maybe one day she'd have her own little girl and they'd play together too.

"Why you smile, Aunt Hayweee?"

"I'm smiling because my heart is filled with love." She tapped her niece's nose as joy filled her. She finally knew what to do without a shadow of doubt.

20

Two weeks after her conversation in the park with Michael, Hailey sat in her office contemplating her next move. Ian had accepted the position she'd offered. In fact he seemed excited about it. Apparently, he enjoyed traveling and dealing one-on-one with customers.

Things were finally settling into a comfortable routine. The staff seemed happy. Trent was back to his regular job and Michael...well she wasn't sure about him. They only talked shop, and she never saw him outside the office anymore. She had to give him credit for backing off and respecting her wishes, but now that things were going smoothly she seriously missed him. She hadn't meant for them to have zero contact outside of work.

Was she a horrible person? She didn't want to be someone who pushed the people she cared about away in times of stress or crisis, yet she'd done that with Michael. She'd even done it with her mom to a certain extent. Leaving after her sister and brother-in-law were killed had been self-preservation, and she didn't regret it, but she was stronger now.

She stood and squared her shoulders then headed across the hall to Michael's office. She stood in the doorway as he spoke to someone on the phone.

"Great, I'll pick you up at seven." He hung up then looked her direction. His face became guarded.

"You have a date?" Was she too late?

"Something like that. What can I do for you?"

Her heart pounded. He'd moved on. "I uh…I—"

"Hailey, I have a lot of work to do. What do you need?" His voice was gentle.

She cleared her throat. She would regret this forever if she didn't speak her mind. "Five minutes."

He sat back in his chair and waved her toward the seat across from his desk.

"Not here."

He shook his head ever so slightly. "What's going on?"

Hailey looked over her shoulder. No one was nearby to overhear. She stepped into his office and closed the door. "Fine. We can talk here." She sat and folded her hands in her lap. "I made a mistake."

He leaned forward slightly, and his brow furrowed. "What kind of mistake?"

"I thought my issue with you was about control. And maybe it was, but the truth of it is, I was doing the same thing in a way. I was so overwhelmed with my new position and responsibilities that I allowed it to control me, and as an act of self-preservation I retreated inward—my own way of gaining control. I'm sorry. It was not the right decision. I see that now."

He nodded. "What are you saying?"

He was going to make her spell it out? She took a breath and let it out slowly. "I'm saying, I don't want you to go out on that date tonight with another woman. I want to be the only woman you date."

A slow grin stretched his cheeks. "Is that so?"

She nodded.

He stood and walked around to her side of the desk. He leaned against it with his ankles crossed and hands in the pockets of his trousers. "As it happens I want the same thing."

Her insides burst with happiness as she jumped up and wrapped her arms around his neck. He shifted so he was standing then wrapped his arms around her waist. She smiled up at him. "Thank you."

"For what?"

"Giving me a second chance and for cancelling your date tonight."

"Oh, I'm not cancelling that. I have to pick someone up from the airport at seven."

She chuckled. "You let me think there was another woman."

He shrugged. "Can you blame me?"

"Not really."

He placed a soft kiss on her lips before releasing her. She stepped back and suddenly remembered they were in his office, which was in essence an oversized fishbowl. Anyone walking by would have seen them. Her face burned. She looked toward the window and breathed easier.

Michael laughed. "Were you worried we'd be caught?"

"Kind of."

He tapped her nose playfully. "I think the entire office is already on to us."

"No!" She jerked her head toward the window. "How?"

"Ian came to me and asked why we were suddenly so frosty toward one another."

Her eyes widened. "What did you say?"

"I denied it."

"Good. But I guess I can see how people would think that since we were so friendly before."

He drew her close. "I'm looking forward to being friendly once again."

She giggled. "Me too."

He dipped his head and captured her lips with a toe-tingling kiss.

Epilogue

Seven months later

Michael stood at the door to Hailey's over-the-garage apartment. She'd decided to stay at her brother's place so she could be close to her nieces and nephew. She'd thoroughly embraced being an aunt.

He slipped his hand into his jacket pocket and felt for the ring he'd had made for Hailey. The white gold band held a karat diamond in the center with smaller diamonds fanning down each side. Maybe it was cheesy to propose on Valentine's Day, but he didn't care. Hailey was the love of his life.

The door flung open and Hailey stood there wearing a red dress that fit her to perfection. Soft ringlets of hair formed around her face, which held a pleasing glow. "I saw you standing here but didn't hear you knock. Come in. Dinner is about ready."

He went inside and followed her to the kitchenette. He'd wanted to take her out on the town, but she'd insisted on cooking. "You look beautiful. Is the dress new?"

She twirled. "I picked it up at a little vintage shop Katie found."

"Nice." He happened to know firsthand she could afford an expensive new dress. The fact she chose to frequent a vintage shop made him love her all the more.

"I'll hang your coat for you." She reached out her hand.

He drew her close and kissed her.

She wrapped her arms around his neck. "That was unexpected."

"I'm full of surprises."

"Sounds intriguing." She gave him a peck then tried to step back.

He stopped her. "I had this all planned out in my mind, but I can't wait." He dropped to one knee and pulled the box from his pocket. Opening the lid, he held it out. "I was smitten with you when we first met, and that attraction has grown with each day I've known you. I love you with all my heart, and I want to spend the rest of my life with you. Will you marry me?"

"Yes!" Hailey pulled him to standing and kissed him soundly before finally releasing him.

He chuckled. "I'm not the only one full of surprises.

Author Note

Thanks for reading *Simply Smitten*. I hope you enjoyed the latest installment in the Brides of Seattle series. Even though this series takes place in a big city, I have had such a fun time creating this story world. I've been to Seattle a few times during the plotting of this series and each time I discover something new. This last trip was for a week, and I stayed in a neighborhood in Ballard. It was nice to get the feel of neighborhood life that was in walking distance to restaurants, a coffee shop, grocery store, and even the water.

As of this moment, I plan to write the third book in this series and publish it sometime in 2019. I still need to decide whom the story will be about, but I'm leaning toward Paige. What do you think? Should Paige have her own story?

I enjoy hearing from readers and have several ways we can connect. The links are below. I hope you join my Facebook Readers Group and subscribe to my newsletter. The Amazon link is for you to be notified whenever one of my books releases.

Finally, if you enjoyed this book, please tell a friend. Word of mouth and writing reviews is the best way you can help me continue to do what I do.

Blessings,
Kimberly Rose Johnson

Subscribe to my newsletter at kimberlyrjohnson.com
Amazon follow: http://amzn.to/2jpZj1C
Facebook: www.facebook.com/KimberlyRoseJohnson

Books by
Kimberly Rose Johnson

Brides of Seattle
The Reluctant Groom
Simply Smitten

Melodies of Love
A Love Song for Kayla
An Encore for Estelle
A Waltz for Amber

Sunriver Dreams
A Love to Treasure
A Christmas Homecoming
Designing Love

Wildflower B&B Romance Series
Island Refuge
Island Dreams
Island Christmas
Island Hope

Contemporary Inspirational Romance Collection
In Love and War

Contemporary Novella
Brewed with Love